Rip's Knickerbockers

Rip's Knickerbockers

LINDEN J. DeBIE

RESOURCE *Publications* · Eugene, Oregon

RIP'S KNICKERBOCKERS

Resource Publications
An Imprint of Wipf and Stock Publishers
199 W. 8th Ave., Suite 3
Eugene, OR 97401

www.wipfandstock.com

PAPERBACK ISBN: 979-8-3852-2765-5
HARDCOVER ISBN: 979-8-3852-2766-2
EBOOK ISBN: 979-8-3852-2767-9

For Cailyn, Nik, and Charlotte Rose

"The story of Rip Van Winkle may seem incredible to many, but nevertheless I give it my full belief, for I know the vicinity of our old Dutch settlements to have been very subject to marvelous events and appearances. Indeed, I have heard many stranger stories than this, in the villages along the Hudson; all of which were too well authenticated to admit of a doubt. I have even talked with Rip Van Winkle myself . . . [and] I have seen a certificate on the subject taken before a country justice, and signed with cross, in the justice's own handwriting. The story, therefore, is beyond the possibility of doubt."

—*Rip Van Winkle* by Washington Irving

Contents

1

The Dutch Catskills, 1776

RIP VAN WINKLE'S SQUIRREL gun gave off a tremendous report, and the unfortunate furry critter fell among the lush Catskill flora. Other than the smell of gunpowder the air was as fresh as a mountain spring. There was a hint of balsam, spearmint, thyme, sage, and beebalm. The fifty-year-old Rip Van Winkle breathed deeply of the fragrances and once again found himself restored. The lingering whiff of gunpowder simply added to his delight. He immediately concluded that only one other smell could improve the air, and he drew out his old clay pipe with its long, curved stem and lit up a bowl.

This morning the delightfully sensuous air was as still as stone, and the cracking sound of the rifle could be heard well south down along the great palisades of the western shore of the Hudson River. It would carry west as far as Paramus, New Jersey, where the wild turkeys flourished. Equally, it would reach eastward to the opposite bank and the bluff where Tarrytown, also called Upper Mills and Sleepy Hallow, were located. This was one of the many Hudson Valley settlements of the people known far and wide as the Knickerbockers for the pants they wore; pants rolled up just below the knee. It was, in fact, the knickers that gave the people their colloquial name, Knickerbockers.

From the hunter's location on this gentle rise on the western bank he could view through the forest canopy the widest section of the river called by the Lenni Lenape and Mahican tribes Mahicantuck, which means "the river that flows two ways." The earliest Dutch traders called them "River Indians" from the time of Columbus who thought he had arrived at the extreme edge of India. And as for the river itself, it was called by the Dutch, Mauritse, and by the English, North River. Later it would take the name of its first English explorer and after 1740 be known as the Hudson River.

It wasn't unusual for Rip to encounter Native American hunting parties on his wanderings, but only if they wanted him to. On this occasion a friendly group of Wickquasgecks surprised him. They traded some tobacco, leather skins, and wampum and then moved down the rise where they left their canoes, returning to the eastern side of the river. The Wickquasgecks, an offshoot of the Mohicans and descendants of the great Algonquian tribes, were the first known inhabitants of the woods around latter-day Tarrytown. But their range was extensive and included the land of White Plains, a name taken from the Indians for the marshes and plains which were often shrouded by a white mist. They fished the Mahicantuck with its abundant schools of shad, and they gathered oysters from its banks where the brackish water pushed north up the river literally making it a river that flowed both ways. All along the Hudson flocks of sandpipers and mergansers populated the marshes. In the water along with the oysters, were mussels and clams, and of course fish of various species. Likewise, the verdant forests which were inhabited by dear, turkey, and squirrel, provided ample game and good soil as long as one kept a wary eye out for black bears, wolves, and mountain lions.

The Wickquasgecks of the lower Hudson subsisted mainly on a river diet supplemented by a little farming. Upriver the native people were more serious about cultivating crops and grew abundant harvests of corn and other staples such as beans and squash. The ambitious Dutch farmers who had never seen many of these exotic fruits and vegetables were eager to learn the farming techniques of the River Indians and enthusiastically participated in trade with them. In fact, it was the native peoples that created the first economic system in North America, one centered around trade, especially in furs, with wampum as the mutually recognized currency. The Dutch simply employed and adjusted that system to meet their needs.

While the Wickquasgecks were nomadic like their kin they typically inhabited that part of the Eastern bank called Alipconk or the Forest of Elms. The Dutch settlers found the area as irresistible as the natives, and they settled in what became known to them as Tarwe (Wheat) Town around 1645 as part of the settlements of New Netherland.

Like the other villages, Tarrytown was sponsored by the colonizing Dutch West India Company. But unlike the more famous colonists of New England who left Europe primarily for religious reasons, the first Dutch settlers were mostly destitute Walloons desirous of a better life and embarked on the dangerous voyage in hopes of future prosperity. This required their cooperation with the native people, even if begrudgingly so. Consequently, it was through commercial and cultural relationships, education, and exchange that the lives of both the native people and the Europeans were transformed into something entirely new and different.

The natives knew of Rip Van Winkel and his rambling ways. More often than not, they detected his presence from the smell of his favorite tobacco, Golden Weed, and even before making out his visage they recognized his tattered homespun knickers and moth-eaten hat with an eagle's feather protruding from the black band. His waistcoat was stained and wrinkled. His boots were weather-beaten, and the soles were worn down to the point they only just kept out the wet. His beard was long and tangled and white like his hair, and his appearance was altogether disheveled. He was tall and lanky. But his face was pleasant with a grin that rarely left him outside of any trouble that he might stir up, especially with his formidable wife. But most folks only knew his cheerful laughter and agreeable disposition.

2

The Island of *Manahatta*, 1609

HENRY HUDSON LEANED ON the parapet and gave out a loud sneeze. Something on this river was teasing his nose. He'd never had issues in Europe, but he was far from Europe now. "I've had a monstrous headache since we entered these waters," he said to his first mate, Robert Juet.

Juet was unsympathetic. "It was a mistake to attack that Indian village. For what, a few pelts and some meager rations? Are we not better than that?"

"Robert, I can only rein in the men to an extent, and unless they are given certain freedoms they will mutiny."

"I simply recommend treating the natives equitably. That is if we want to survive this voyage," was Juet's frank reply.

It was early September 1609 and Hudson was the captain of the three-masted carrack the *Half Moon* (in the Dutch *Halve Maen*) when it sailed into what is now called Upper New York Bay. The ship was owned by the Muscovy Company. "If there is a passage to India it will be here, upriver, or a river farther north," Hudson confided to Juet. But we must consider every possibility, and in the meantime map all that we explore. Successful or not, the company is sure to capitalize on whatever we find here."

"Aye, sir," Juet nodded in agreement. "Are you sure you gave enough attention to the great bay and river south of us?" Juet was speaking of what would come to be known as the Delaware.

"Every seafaring bone in my body tells me that river is not an option," replied Hudson. "First of all, there were the dangerous shallows and sandbars, and the river was simply too shallow and inconsistent. No, that's not the Northwest Passage, I'm sure of it. But before us . . . I wonder?"

The *Half Moon* continued north, its crew marveling at the sheer magnitude of the coastline. As they rounded a white sand coastal hook they saw what appeared to be three rivers flowing into a huge, sheltered bay. They anchored near a great white sand hook, and a party of five took a rowboat to scout the area.

"Keep tight to the banks," ordered John Colman, second mate of the *Half Moon* and leader of the scouting party. They sought to work their way north just above the wetlands where they could step onto dry ground and have a look around, but before they got there they were surprised. Emerging from the tall reeds just south of the hook were five Lenape canoes filled with warriors. "Don't fire, there's too many of them, just make haste for the ship," was Colman's order. But the swift canoes gained on the small boat, and when the natives were close enough they loosed their arrows and Colman was shot through the neck severing an artery. He bled out in short order. Two others were wounded. When the rowboat neared the much larger ship the native canoes retreated back into the marshes without a shot being fired.

"Tough break," said Juet. "He was a good sailor."

"We'll bury him on the hook. It's a fitting resting place," said the captain. "Have Cookie carve a suitable marker, he's the best whittler we got."

The next day they hugged the shore along present-day New Jersey until they reached the palisades, enormous, great walls of volcanic diabase stone. Finally spotting an especially pleasant tree-lined shore on the western coast of New Jersey, they went ashore to explore. Especially wary after their previous encounter, they went heavily armed. Amidst stately oaks and an abundance of fruits and berries of various kinds, they were suddenly surrounded, this time by friendly and peaceful people dressed in skins offering them corn and tobacco. Neither spoke such that they understood each other, but in the way of these things, through a lot of pointing, smiling, hand signals, and nodding, they were able to trade. For the next few days, the ship explored the marshes, inlets, rivers, islands, and bays around New Jersey and Staten Island. Having investigated Upper Bay, Hudson took the ship north anticipating the discovery that would make him famous.

"Juet," Hudson called his first mate to him. "Take a sounding. My guess is the river has the size and depth necessary for a passage to Asia."

Juet confirmed his captain's instincts. The size of the river and its depth led them both to believe this could indeed be the fabled route to the Indian Subcontinent. As they traveled upriver they discovered more natives living in round wooden huts made of tree bark. Cautious and well-armed they anchored near some of the native canoes that came out to meet them in hopes of resupplying their provisions. While the crew remained on board and on high alert, the canoes with traders and goods freely pulled alongside the ship. Several came aboard uninvited, but the crew found them peaceful and hospitable. Juet again recommended dealing fairly with their new friends and Hudson agreed. Each having made their offers and with mutual approval, the canoes returned to the shore and the *Half Moon* continued upriver. But then the *Mahicantuck* grew narrow, and the captain and crew had to abandon any hope of finding a passage to India.

"No choice but to turn around," Hudson commanded Juet.

But Juet was alarmed. "It may be too late. The river has narrowed considerably, and our draft is but a few feet. This far upriver there's no tide to speak of, so waiting won't help."

"No, no waiting," replied the captain. "We haven't any choice unless you want to die in this desolate wilderness." Hudson was visibly annoyed. "You will have to turn her around as best you can. So, get us out of here, and you can finally earn your keep."

And so, with difficulty, they turned the ship around and began the return journey south, found themselves in more clashes with the natives, and on a rainy night they silently sailed past an island on the lower, eastern side of the river called *Mannahata* or "hilly island." "What do you make of that?" Hudson asked his first mate.

"Might be worth further exploration," Juet replied.

"No time for it now," Hudson countered. "Just record your general observations and let it be." Then he ordered the ship home having failed in their ultimate quest. However, the journey was by no means a complete failure. The Dutch government laid claim to a vast swath of the new continent which encompassed three great systems of rivers including the Delaware to the South, the Connecticut to the North, and of course the Hudson. Plans were now coming together to colonize and exploit the New World.

The sense among many in the Netherlands (it was likewise the case with all the European powers) was that the motherland needed to take hold of this enormous territory and civilize it in the name of their religion, in the Dutch case, Calvinism, and the interests of the state, but also for the profit that might be gained. That in turn led to the creation of the Dutch West India Company. Their goal was to settle people in the territories explored by Hudson and beyond and secure a hold in the New World in order to begin the exportation of goods from the colony they would call New Netherland. So, roughly four years after the former company's sponsorship of the voyage of Hudson, a ship named the *Nieu Netherlandt* crewed by low-Dutch colonists left Amsterdam and made for the river originally discovered in 1524 by the Florentine navigator Giovanni da Verrazano. Upon landing, the skipper, Cornelis May, became the provisional commander of the colony.

The first young and desperate settlers were Walloons who came during the years 1624 and 1625 in groups of tens and twenties aboard an unlikely assortment of barely seaworthy vessels, bringing along their livestock and the few possessions they had. It could take as much as four months to make the voyage and, if lucky, as little as three. Steering wide of the dangerous islands inhabited by the enemies of the Dutch, as well as the ferocious buccaneers and raiders who patrolled the waters off the continent of America, they kept watch for that same sandy hook first described to them by the crew of the Half Moon.

Ships with such hopeful names as the *Fortune* deposited their passengers and cargo on a wide berth of territory according to William Murray's rule "possession is nine-tenths of the law." While the English considered first discovery a legitimate claim to ownership, the Dutch insisted that ownership was established by inhabiting the land. But the problem with the Dutch scheme of scattering their colonists over extensive tracts of land was that it did little for security. The Dutch would soon discover that they would not be able to control their territory with so few people. The English, Swedes, and native people, among others, would challenge Dutch claims to the land, often by war.

"It was about time the company sent us the materials we need to build decent homes." It was the second provisional director of the colony, Willem Verhulst, speaking to Bastiaen Krol about the miserable earthen dugout and bark-covered hovels the colonists were forced to live in. Pastor Krol had made the journey south from Fort Orange to lead religious services at Nut Island, the first settlement on the eastern shore of the lower Hudson, a small island directly across from *Manahatta*. Krol was pleased to know the colonists would finally have better quarters.

The lay minister was the first pastor of the colony. The two other bystanders to Verhulst's outburst were Joris Rapalje and his teenage wife, Catalina Trico, who married just before their departure from the Netherlands. Joris echoed the sentiments of the director, "We've all had enough indeed of living and sleeping in these dreadful huts. We must continue to make it a priority to get the colony's houses built."

"Indeed," replied Verhulst, "And they will provide better protection from the savages." The attitude and sentiment of Verhulst would prove to be his undoing.

The company had placed Verhulst in charge of the settlement on Nut Island without proper vetting. Now called Governors

Island, it stood directly across from the southern tip of the island the natives called *Manahatta*. Almost immediately violence with the locals erupted, and Verhulst was the instigator. In his greed, he was caught red-handed cheating the Indians in spite of direct orders from the West India Company to treat the natives well and deal honestly with them. It led to an Indian uprising and serious bloodshed. Naturally, the colonists wanted Verhulst gone, and soon a French-speaking Walloon named Peter Minuit was appointed commander. Under Minuit's leadership it was agreed that Nut Island was too small to meet their needs, so the colony decided to explore the Island of *Manahatta*.

It was early summer 1626 when the relocating colonist landed on the southern tip of *Manahatta*, a tree-lined shore resplendent in poplars, oaks, chestnuts, and elms and began their building of what would become one of the greatest cities in the world, calling it New Amsterdam.

Soon they were met by a contingent of the inhabitants of the island along with their leader or *Sackima*. Once again, the game of hand signals and body language somehow led to a deal. The nearby village was populated by 200 to 300 people, a branch of the Lenni Lenape tribes. But the visit was by no means random nor was it without formality. If a European colony was to be established on *Manahatta* it would be by way of a binding treaty, and the Indians insisted on a consummating ceremony including a record on parchment paper that the two would mutually ratify, along with the requisite feasting, drinking, and exchanging of gifts necessary to satisfy both parties. The price, sixty Dutch guilders, which is typically spoken of in island lore, was the approximate worth of the Dutch offering.

Of course, the deal struck convinced the Dutch that they had purchased *Manahatta* and could occupy it and oversee the construction of the village of New Amsterdam. What the colonists did not know but would later come to realize, was that the islanders were simply entering into a treaty by which the two would share the land and become allies in trade and protecting each other's interests, and that included coming to each other's aid in case of war with hostile tribes. There was no talk of ownership, nor could there be, as the natives could not fathom the concept of private property.

Later this became obvious to the settlers when it turned out that they would be responsible for hosting the visits of their new neighbors, oftentimes unannounced. They soon discovered they were expected to demonstrate obligatory hospitality of shelter, food, beer, and brandy for the *Sackimas*. And as the years went by and as the village became the city of New Amsterdam, the citizens who by then were from all parts of the world found themselves frequented by the native people. These would habitually camp out wherever they pleased and trade, interact, and occasionally drink with whomever they encountered. The result was that relations with the native people were sketchy and at times violent. Both sides were capable of atrocities, and both suffered from men who valued power over peace. But when it came to larceny the Europeans would take the lead and teach the Indians avarice.

Most of the violent struggles were indeed between the Dutch and the Indians. Again, the Dutch entered into treaties with the various tribes thinking they bought the land, and that they could safely build towns and expand their property. Rather, from the natives' point of view, it primarily meant that they became trading partners and allies in defense of one another. To enter into a treaty with a tribe meant that the Dutch became the enemy of the tribe's enemies.

3

A Man and His Dog, 1776

RIP'S BLAST HAD THE dogs on the West bank responding with incessant barking unaware that the hunter was miles away. So clear and quiet were these old hills that day that were it not for Wolf's repulsion from excitement, the other dogs would have set him off as well, off on a barking spree that could last an hour or more.

Wolf was Rip's beloved hound and constant companion. But they were more than just companions, rather soul mates and as such, they shared many of the same traits. Just like Rip Wolf was averse to turmoil and labor of any kind, hunting never being considered anything but sport. Neither did much running confident that a brisk walk accomplished the same end. They both adored children and while Wolf could not smoke with the enthusiasm of Rip and his fellow Knickerbockers, he had gnawed to pieces enough clay and wood pipes to have grown fond of the taste of tobacco and charcoal. But mostly they loved to sleep and never missed an opportunity for a long nap. They would have slept more often were it not for Dame Van Winkle's incessant harangue. But here again, Rip and Wolf shared the practice of avoiding Katrina as much as possible. And while she seemed to enjoy swatting the old hound for pure pleasure, she confined herself to the occasional boxing of Rip's ears and left it there. Her tongue was as sharp as her chin, and her nose had the look of a bird's beak. She appeared as formidable as she was. Her voice could shave a dog's hair and cut off a man's legs at the knees, and no one in the village could understand how a quiet and laconic layabout like Rip Van Winkle ended up with such a bedmate.

The two had a son and a younger daughter, the girl taking after her mother in diligence and not so in attitude. Indeed, she was rather charitable and sweet. The son was the image of his father with his father's carefree ways. Lazy and always adrift, he was the target of his mother's bite, yet he seemed oblivious. He neither challenged her nor did he obey her. He simply ignored her.

But this morning man and dog kept such thoughts as far behind them as the village while the sun of a perfect day insisted that nothing spoil it. The morning was so pleasant Rip couldn't decide if he was more interested in hunting or simply traversing the numerous Indian trails and countless tributaries. Thus, he reasoned to do both, and off the two went along one of the many footpaths of the mountain forest.

Rather, these were old hills, not the mountains of the lands far to the west. Worn down by thousands and thousands of years of erosion, the Catskills were part of the greater Appalachian Mountain range. They could not match the grandeur much less the altitude of the ranges like the Rockies. No, their glory was found elsewhere, in the lush richness of their antiquity which had flourished in centuries of natural development. Only the people of the forest, the people the Knickerbockers referred to as "savages," knew its secrets and its mystery. Yet the Dutch who had ventured into this new world typically respected the vast woodlands and the resourceful, practical people who inhabited them. And while they were given to demeaning epithets such as "barbarians," quixotically most of them respected the natives for their natural gifts and their reverence for the forest's majesty.

Another well-placed shot accounted for the fourth nicely fattened rodent for Rip's small game bag. Enough for a decent stew for his family with leftovers for old Wolf. Maybe just enough incentive to curb the harsh tongue of his tempestuous wife whose talent at finding fault was unsurpassed in the little, unnamed Dutch village from which they came.

4

The Founding
of New Amsterdam, 1626

As ODD AS THE behavior of the Indians appeared to the colonists it certainly proved equally so for the natives. It simply became a fact of their co-existence. It was the natives who taught the Dutch how to construct the dugout cellar-like shelters they first inhabited. In time the colonists stepped up their trade and exports and built two windmills, one for producing grain and the other for lumber. Minuit had also erected a sturdy stone structure as the headquarters of the Dutch West India Company, and as for the colony's defenses a ramshackle fort was built on the southwest tip of the island complete with a chapel inside for worship.

As materials arrived from the Netherlands and elsewhere more permanent wooden structures were built. Nor was a single plan for the seaport town agreed to, so New Amsterdam came about spontaneously with roads simply following old Indian trails or the paths created by cows and pigs going from farm to field. With better materials the settlement graduated to small wooden houses built near the river as waterfront homes. In time the wooden houses and buildings gave way to larger structures built of brick or stone based on Dutch architecture. By 1664 these buildings were typically made of brick. Eventually, a plan called the Costello Plan was approved by the company. It followed the more haphazard development of the town, but it determined what now would be its urban character.

Governed for the single purpose of profit and allowing as little self-rule as possible, the outpost was never intended by the Dutch West India Company as a city but rather a company town, and the inhabitants were more employees than citizens. As such, their job was to see to it that the company turned a profit for their investors. Indeed, the directors in Amsterdam applied enormous pressure on Minuit and the colony to deliver, and they insisted it must be as profitable as their Caribbean salt plantations. However, the main commodity early on was fir, especially bever pelts. But the plan for the future was to exploit all the resources of the new world. The grand idea was to model New Netherland after the profitability of the East Indies and so duplicate the colonialism and unabashed imperialism that had brought them financial wealth. The Dutch business leaders' scheme envisioned lucrative plantations led by company employees and worked by slave labor. Nevertheless, it was a model being employed by all the great powers of Europe at the time. The point was to make the rulers rich.

Understandably, the result of financial governance by a distant board was the absence of a coherent policy for civil behavior. There were no laws, not to speak of, other than what they might refer back to as what was done in the Netherlands. Law by established precedent. When something unusual roiled the community appointed burger meisters would sit in judgment, smoke their pipes, and decide in the manner of a pragmatic casuistry not unlike the earliest judges of Israel.

This was in stark contrast to the Pilgrim and Puritan settlements of New England. At the time of Minuit, the New England Pilgrim colony struggled and barely managed to survive. Nor did they show much interest in becoming a commercial success owing no fidelity, hence financial obligation, to the kings and queens of Europe. The mindset was deeply ingrained in them, and this was exhibited throughout New England as the very spirit of Puritan culture. Theirs was a theocracy governed by strict religious oversight by their pastors. Thus, New England's identity was cast in a disciplined, austere zeal, piety, and religious stoicism of the Calvinistic brand. Ironically, this was the same religion promoted by the Dutch West India Company, and the only faith legally recognized in New Netherland. However, religion aside, the Dutch did not give themselves over to the religious enthusiasm of New England, whose aspirations were to build the kingdom of God on the new continent. These would be cities based on the Gospel and free from interference by the established churches of Europe.

Lodged literally and culturally between the pious Puritan North and the growing commercial city of New Amsterdam to the south were the Dutch villages and towns dotted along the Hudson River and scattered among the territories of New Netherland. Further east were the farms of Long Island and to the west the settlements of New Jersey. And of course, there were the towns growing up in what would become the boroughs of later-day New York City. Although these early settlers who typically made their living by farming were brought over from the Netherlands to fulfill the commercial interests of the West India Company, many, especially in the rural villages, entertained an entirely different agenda from their masters. Soon their independence from the company would become insured by the loss of New Netherland to the British, but that only gave support to their deeper desire to recreate the culture of the Netherlands in the New World.

Although New Amsterdam was rapidly becoming an international port, the Dutch culture dominated. Soon the fort was surrounded by small Dutch-style homes with tiled roofs with weathercocks. An enclosure of palisades served as protection for the settlers. Stretching out from there were farms with their fields of corn, cabbage, and of course, the essential crop for Dutch civilization, tobacco. These stretched as far as latter-day Broadway, Wallstreet, and Pearl Street.

In those early days of the colony the common dress was modestly comprised mostly of traditional homespun. The women wore small caps of quilted calico. Petticoats made of linsey-woolsey were gayly striped with multiple colors reaching just below the knees. They had several pockets in place of a bag for things needed

15

at hand, and colorful ribbons were tied to useful items such as scissors and pincushions. Their typically blue worsted stockings gave way to leather shoes boasting enormous silver buckles.

The men wore the linsey-woolsey galligaskins made by their wives. But as New Amsterdam grew more prosperous the showier man would wear a linsey-woolsey coat with several large brass buttons. Below the coat were his breeches and leather shoes with great copper buckles, and above he sported a broad-brimmed hat. His hair was long, and a pipe was typically in his mouth.

Issues of fashion, however, were foreign to the simple tastes of Rip Van Winkle whose disheveled appearance suited his character. As the sun was intent on setting soon, Rip and Wolf reluctantly turned onto a familiar deer path leading to the quiet Catskill village on the banks of the Hudson they called home. Shortly he could see tiny columns of smoke, and due to the stillness of the air the smoke languidly rose from the Dutch chimneys. The village sprouted about the time of the short tenure of the renowned seaman and director general of New Amsterdam, Peter Stuyvesant. Stuyvesant was the last of a short list of early colonial governors all in the pay of the Dutch West India Company.

5

Trouble In Paradise, 1627

BY 1627 THE COLONISTS of New Amsterdam had about thirty wooden homes built along the southeastern shore of the Hudson River, along with the sturdy stone structure of the Dutch West India Company. Shortly a duly ordained domine or pastor arrived by the name of Jonas Michaelius, and although called to bring comfort to his new flock he was contentious, bitter, and domineering.

"I yearn for the day my contract expires in three years," he complained to his two young daughters. The pastor may have had reason to be jaded having lost his pregnant and sickly wife on the voyage.

"I cannot abide these wretched people. In most ways, they're not much better than the heathens and savages that run amok here. And as for that devil Minuit and his plans to carve up New Netherland, no doubt he's scheming to give the colony to those greedy directors and would-be patroons back home. As if shipping over hundreds of colonists and handing them over to wealthy, undeserving plantation owners would ensure the success of the colony. No, I say, it will only divide us further and leave each part of New Netherland unprotected. Well, he won't get away with it. Not if I have anything to say about it. Mark my words, the more rational directors in Holland will know of his betrayal through my letters."

In those letters the angry cleric falsely branded Minuit a villain and schemer seeking to cheat the directors out of their investment. But Michaelius's correspondence was incendiary and compelling enough to have both he and Minuit recalled to the Netherlands. It was a cloudy, dark day in 1632 when Minuit, frothing at the mouth and indignant, joined his adversary on board the ship ironically named *Unity* for their voyage back to the Netherlands. They would share close quarters during the two-month journey. The case was heard, and in spite of no evidence of maleficence and, in fact, a rather stellar progress report, Minuit was dismissed. Later he would die in a shipwreck off the Caribbean. Lay pastor Krol was left in charge for the time being.

This did not bode well for the colony which had grown under Minuit's leadership. Now it was as if the colony had been cut adrift. Making matters worse an indecisive and weak director, Wouter van Twiller, replaced Krol in 1638. He likely got the job through family connections, and the company looked aside at his excessive drinking because of his devotion to them. He was bent on carrying out West India's mandate that New Netherland be a prosperous trading post. However, the island city had already become much more than that. Indeed, it was rapidly becoming a famous world port destined to play a major role in global politics.

But under van Twiller New Amsterdam was falling apart. When the company realized its mistake they appointed Wilhelm Kieft director in 1638. He was a greedy, violent man who hated the native people.

"Look, the whole point of this miserable venture is to make the company and us rich. The savages would just as soon smoke our tobacco and drink our rum as benefit from white culture. And we have the guns and determination to keep them in their place, and their place is at our heels."

Kieft was confiding in a Spanish mercenary, Manuel Cortez, who had taken up with the Dutch having grown too old for life at sea. He became indispensable to Kieft and did his dirty work for him.

"The tax scheme we dreamed up should have been sufficient, but the Indians aren't paying up. And yesterday I got word that it might have been some of these deadbeat savages that stole a bunch of pigs from old David de Vries. True or not we're gonna pin it on 'em. Round up a dozen of those scurvy villains you associate with, and take them down to Corlears Hook and do what you have to do."

"Aye sir, you know you can count on me." Cortez enjoyed violence as much as he enjoyed his rum.

He took with him twenty drunken ex-pirate associates and slaughtered a number of innocent native women and children. This was followed by other atrocities perpetrated by soldiers under Kieft's command. The result was a rare unification of serval tribes against the Dutch. This time it was the natives who brought retribution to the colony as instigated by the union of tribes.

The Indian War or Kieft's War, as it was called, not only left the colony in disorder but people were dying, and many farmers were displaced and forced to take refuge in the fort. Instead of backing off Kieft doubled down. However, thanks to the skill of a Leiden-trained lawyer, Adriaen Van der Donck, a persuasive letter of complaint was spirited off to the company directors in Amsterdam. It contained rare language for those times, words about representative government and human rights. But instead of taking sides with the colonists, the company men in Amsterdam decided to sack Kieft and bring in a strongman, a no-nonsense administrator. Their choice was Peter Stuyvesant.

Stuyvesant arrived in New Amsterdam in 1647 with the idea of establishing a military-style dictatorship and the promise to "govern them like a father." It may be that a strong but diplomatic leader was necessary given the chaos of the colony. He had made a name for himself in several famous battles, one in which he lost his right leg. He was a well-built, physical kind of man with a commanding voice often given to outbursts of emotion. However, his governing style was simple and straightforward as he typically avoided the advice of others always confident he was right. Still, harassment of the Indians continued and would create problems for Stuyvesant who although he thought them savages, had strict orders from the company to treat them equitably.

Another thorn in his flesh was the fort the Swedes had established on the Dutch-held South River later called the Delaware, where they entered into a treaty with the native people. When Stuyvesant dislodged the Swedes the natives felt obligated to retaliate with what was called the Peach War. In its aftermath the director was committed to settling scores, and he did so with considerable diplomatic skill. It began to appear as if order would, at last, be restored to the colony. In part, this was due to the cessation of hostilities with the Indians, and after the Peach War Dutch military actions essentially ended native control of the region.

Stuyvesant's other headache was created by an internal crisis. While the early chaos of the colony evaporated in a surge of commercial expansion during the late 1640s after which the colony experienced its greatest population growth, the old enemies of Kieft saw an opportunity to press their agenda of a more representative government and greater liberty. Several of them were members of a board of elected representatives, and they were growing in power and independence. Stuyvesant would see to it that such radical ideas were crushed.

But perhaps his major concern was with New England who with the support of England continued to have designs on New Netherland. Their intrusion into the affairs of the colony was such that Stuyvesant could not afford to ignore them. The seriousness of the situation was amplified by the fact that English ambitions came from the very top, from none other than King Charles I who sought in every way possible to curb the growth of Dutch trade throughout the expanding world, as well as to lay hands on the entirety of the new continent.

It was not lost on Stuyvesant that England had long had its eye on New Amsterdam. Indeed, English lawyers argued that the ship that claimed the island of *Manahatta*, the *Half Moon*, sailed out from the Chesapeake near the English plantation of North Virginia and thus was under English jurisdiction. Moreover, they insisted that the purchase of *Manahatta* was illegal as the Indians had no claim to the island. Finally, they contended that with the earlier landing of the Englishman, John Cabot, in Newfoundland, all the unclaimed territory stretching out from there to the north, the south, and the west could be claimed for England. However, about that same time, in 1649, Charles I was beheaded, and civil war brought a temporary halt to England's aspirations for the new world.

Now it was only with New England that Stuyvesant had to contend. But rather than go to war, he managed to negotiate a treaty guaranteeing the Dutch rights to the largest tracts of New Netherland including Manhattan and its diamond in the rough, New Amsterdam. The New Englanders were granted the frontier outposts they had founded and the land on both sides of the Connecticut River. For the time being, New England was pacified and left New Amsterdam alone.

However, although Stuyvesant temporarily managed to calm tensions with New England his administration was in revolt. The impatient board was pressing hard for expanded powers, and Stuyvesant was refusing to accede to their demands. This culminated in a legal effort by the board to oust Stuyvesant, which required that representatives from both parties appear before the Lords States General of the United Netherlands in the Hague. The Lords States functioned as the national parliament of the United Provinces of the Netherlands. Led by the deft hand of Adriaen Van der Donck the board's case won the day, and the States General wrote a letter recalling Stuyvesant. Exuberant, Van der Donck was charged with delivering the letter to the sacked director in person.

And then the unexpected happened all due effectively to one man, Oliver Cromwell. Cromwell's military successes brought the Puritan Revolution to power in England leading to the creation of the British Commonwealth. In 1653 he was named Lord Protector and took full control of England, Scotland, and Ireland. From the moment he came to power he was determined to break the back of the Dutch West India Company, declaring that British ships alone could service British ports. Of course, that included New England but also the English settlements on the American continent, as well as the Caribbean. But Cromwell fully intended to extend the ban to the ports of New Netherland.

When Dutch vessels sailing through the English Channel were ordered to lower their flags in acknowledgment of British sovereignty they refused, and a monumental naval battle commenced leaving both fleets heavily damaged. This set off the first Anglo-Dutch War, a war over trade.

The effect of the crisis was that the attention of the Netherlands turned toward securing victory. New Amsterdam's lawsuit against Stuyvesant was quickly forgotten, and the Dutch West India Company with its years of experience in naval warfare was given new life. With renewed and expanding powers the company expressed dismay over the radical reforms represented by the New Amsterdam board. They insisted such ideas would undermine the war effort. Consequently, the recall of Stuyvesant was rescinded, and Van der Donck was denied permission to leave the Netherlands.

Although the States General knew that New Amsterdam was in imminent danger of an English invasion, they had a war to win and settled for an order that Stuyvesant improve the colony's defenses. Yet they did little to supply the colony with the means to do that. Still, they were correct about English ambitions, and in 1659 Cromwell sent a squadron of ships to capture New Amsterdam. However, before the ships arrived another ship from London came into port bringing news of a peace agreement between the Dutch and the English. Stuyvesant breathed a sigh of relief on both counts, English withdrawal and his restored authority in the city.

Tensions eased and business continued to boom in the growing cosmopolitan city of New Amsterdam. Indeed, business was becoming what the city was all about. In fact, although Stuyvesant and the company were technically in charge, it was the businessmen who were increasingly determining the city's future. The cosmopolitan character of New Amsterdam was evident in the flourishing commercial atmosphere. And as for the Dutch model of business success, a modicum of tolerance was necessary. That would characterize the city of New Amsterdam from the beginning. But initially, it was only a modicum. Tolerance, while soon to become a major aspect of enlightened thinking, was still a nascent idea undeveloped and begrudgingly accepted for the sake of business success. This had implications on a number of levels. In what must be seen as a progressive trajectory the people of New Amsterdam increasingly accepted the growing diversity of their city.

As for the slave issue the Dutch were as guilty as New England and the Southerners, and they kept slaves but not in identical ways. They had before all others established a list of rights, hardly egalitarian but progressive for the time. Provision was made for enslaved people to acquire their freedom, and there were sanctions about their treatment, as well as listed punishments for the illegal treatment of the African people. Some were allowed to work for wages, raise their own crops, own property, marry, raise children, and bring lawsuits against Europeans. Nevertheless, the brutality of the institution was as evident in the Dutch mistreatment of Africans as it was among the Puritan North and the Southern colonies and plantations.

Likewise, freedom of religious expression was allowed but only within limits. Unless you were of the Reformed faith you could not proselytize, nor could you worship openly. Those not of the Reformed religion found it hard to obtain land, and non-Calvinists were harassed by Stuyvesant whose desire was that the Reformed faith be the established religion of the continent. In essence and with certain distinctions, New England was of the same mindset.

Equally so, if New England had their wish Stuyvesant's desire for intolerance would be realized throughout the New World. But the English colonies would never accept that the motley city of New Amsterdam qualified as a model of Reformed orthodoxy. Not Stuyvesant's fault but true enough. Although sharing a similar theology, New England felt no obligation to tolerate non-Puritan religions even of the Reformed variety. Indeed, Britain's and New England's plot to undermine Dutch presence in the New World was being prosecuted by the nephew of a former ally of Stuyvesant,

George Downing, an Anglo-Irish diplomat from the Colony of Connecticut.

But suddenly Downing was forced to contend with an unexpected series of events. Great Britain had once again changed religions. With the death of Cromwell and the return of the Stuarts to the English throne, England was reestablished as Anglican with strong ties to Roman Catholicism. Naturally, that went contrary to the desires of Downing and all of Puritan New England. Nevertheless, they would have to learn to live with the hated episcopacy. But as united as they were in theology and in their animosity toward the established Church of England, the reforming zeal of the New England colonies could not settle issues of authority and territorial control among themselves. As a result, they were constantly at each other's throats.

In hopes of securing his colony's ambitions, Downing traveled to London to obtain recognition of Connecticut, and not only did he achieve his goal, but King Charles II essentially deleted the Massachusetts colony from the map, giving Downing all of the Dutch territories and more. Without really any sense of the enormity of the continent, Charles granted Connecticut ownership of all that lay west to the Pacific Ocean.

Meanwhile, Downing was undermining Stuyvesant. Downing was surely a cad and his politics underhanded. In fact, Stuyvesant was duped. In spite of assurances to the contrary, upon returning from a trip to Fort Orange Stuyvesant was met by four English gunships in New York Harbor. The fort was completely outnumbered and outgunned.

"What are we up against?" Stuyvesant asked Johannes de Decker a West India Company lawyer.

"Well, this is clearly a violation of our rights and of Dutch sovereignty over the colony," the downcast attorney replied.

"I'm not talking about legalities. The British don't give a farthing about Dutch rights, otherwise they wouldn't be here. I'm talking about militarily. What are we up against militarily?" Stuyvesant was exhibiting one of his frequent emotional outbursts.

"What difference does it make? We can't possibly stand against them," Decker was beside himself.

"We stand or we die," Stuyvesant calmed himself. "Now what are we up against?"

"Four British warships all with heavy canon. I would estimate they have a thousand men at their disposal. Not to mention the soldiers marching from Long Island. We have preliminary reports that they have already opened fire on some of our Dutch troops. For our side we have five hundred soldiers, a fort in disrepair, we are desperately low on gunpowder, and our cannons are such that they might explode when lit."

"Good." Stuyvesant calmly replied.

"Good, what's good about it?"

Stuyvesant was grim but determined. "No, good that we know the facts."

"The facts are we will be slaughtered if we resist."

"We shall see," said Stuyvesant. "Take a letter."

It was short and to the point. "What are the intentions of the British in the harbor?"

Captain Nicholls aboard the *Guinea* replied the next morning. Speaking on behalf of the king, he demanded the full surrender of the city along with its forts, buildings, and provisions to the British, and failing that the director could expect a bloody war he could not possibly win.

Stuyvesant returned the letter to Nicholls saying he could not accept it because it was unsigned. Nicholls immediately spirited off a signed letter with the former letter enclosed and the explanation that it was unsigned due to the haste required. He also said he had nothing to add.

"What, Mister de Decker, is our obligation to the company?" Stuyvesant's was a loaded question. De Decker answered, "Nothing."

"It is to fight and win or die trying," Stuyvesant bellowed.

A messenger interrupted the argument. "Director Stuyvesant, there is a launch nearing the fort. It has raised the white flag."

"Then by all means make them welcome and prepare the tavern for a parley."

Aboard the boat was the conniving younger John Winthrop, governor of Massachusetts along with several New Englanders. They were led to the tavern where they joined Stuyvesant, de Decker, a few soldiers, and some of Stuyvesant's staff but no board members.

"Your Excellency and my old friend, I plead with you not to shed Christian blood for a cause you cannot possibly hope to win." Winthrop played the role of the wise and trusted counselor, while Stuyvesant knew all along he was a snake in the grass.

As Stuyvesant grimaced Winthrop continued. "I have seen to it that the terms of the British are generous, and their demands better than you might expect."

Stuyvesant read the letter and instead of being relieved at the generous terms he grew red in the face. He surely realized that the conditions were so generous he would not be able to convince his people to resist. He stared menacingly at Winthrop and barked, "I expect nothing short of the removal from this colony of those invaders in your company who are trespassing." The stubborn director was adamant. "Yet, I am obliged to speak to my board which meets this evening at City Hall."

When the meeting commenced Stuyvesant was surrounded by a mob unwilling to resist the British including Stuyvesant's young son, Balthazar. They demanded to see the terms being offered by the British. But Stuyvesant simply tore the letter to pieces.

The room burst into chaos. "Stuyvesant, are you mad?" It was Domine Megapolensis, the elder. "Why must we die for a company that has shown us nothing but contempt, a company seeking solely its own welfare?" Meanwhile, a board member was pasting together the shredded letter. Once done he read the terms.

Again, the room burst into disarray. It was Megapolensis who silenced the mob and finally spoke. "These terms are generous to the point of benevolence. There is no future for a cause that would bring us to war. We are at their mercy, and yet they show us mercy. Director General, we beg you to surrender the city."

At that, Stuyvesant left City Hall and made for the fort. He climbed the rampart and was about to order the cannon lit. Megapolenisis and his son followed behind and then climbed the stairs to stand beside the stubborn director. The senior pastor spoke quietly in his ear. Then the three descended the rampart. But the irascible director general wasn't finished.

"De Decker, take a letter and address it to Commander Nicholls." The letter reminded Nicholls of Dutch sovereignty over New Netherland, and that were he to check back with the authorities in London he might find he was making a grave mistake.

Meanwhile, the entire city signed a petition addressed to the director to surrender the city. Stuyvesant was livid. "The whole lot of them are spineless traitors," he shouted at de Decker. "The depravity of this decadent mix of religions and races has erased not only their loyalty but their principles. Let me die with my sword in hand." He paced the floor as his son stared at him defiantly. "And yet," moaned the beleaguered director, "what can the brave stand of one loyal man accomplish?"

So, without a shot being fired, the city of New Amsterdam was turned over to the British, and a new name for the city, New York, paid tribute to the fondness King Charles II had for his brother James, the Duke of York.

On what was the fourth day of the standoff, Stuyvesant and his soldiers vacated the fort and removed themselves to his farm. With that he appointed a committee of six to negotiate the terms that would become the Articles of Capitulation. Richard Nicholls, the commander in charge of the invading force replaced Stuyvesant as governor and gracefully accepted the articles.

Consequently, Nicholls continued the novel respect for personal rights as well as the liberal commercial policies of the city including resuming trade with their former enemy. It was an essential practical move. The disruption that would have followed the ouster of Dutch bureaucrats would return the city to chaos and endanger its ongoing profitability. For all intents and purposes this meant that New York was neither Dutch nor English but both. Again, Stuyvesant proved himself a deft negotiator, and his chosen delegation for the transfer of the colony led by de Decker hammered out the terms which, in those days, were a rare declaration of the rights and privileges of the citizens of New York.

While the takeover of New Amsterdam was inevitable and bloodless the States General of the Netherlands were furious and bent on retaliation. Dutch ships embarked on several successful missions capturing English outposts and plantations which led to the Second Anglo-Dutch War. And although the English sued for peace the Dutch failed to recover the colony of New Netherland.

The States General remained mortified and in 1669 they sent a Dutch fleet to attack English Caribbean settlements as well as raiding along the American coastline. Then in 1673 it sailed into New York Harbor and demanded the surrender of the fort. Within days a new Dutch administration took over the city. New York now became New Orange. Strangely, however, under the terms of the later peace settlement the Dutch returned the city to the English and, of course, the city was once again New York.

New York long since ceased to be ethnically monolithic, and the multiethnic makeup simply accelerated its growing diversity. Still, the Dutch stamp on the city was indelible. It was the Dutch system that created the scout which later became the district attorney's office revolutionizing local government as well as increasing efficiency. On the other hand, the Anglo-Dutch wars fueled Great Britain's general disdain for the people of the Netherlands. The effect was a love/hate relationship between the two. This, in turn, led to a predominately English narrative about the founding of America, one that made New England the source of its cultural identity.

In 1712 a revolt of the enslaved resulted in a hardline position on slavery reversing the growing trend toward broadening their rights. It also coincided with a huge increase in the number of enslaved people. At the time of the revolt the number of enslaved was 970 in New York City, three times the number in all of New Netherland. That number would soar to more than 1,500 during the 1730s, which amounted to one in five people being enslaved.

6

A Catskill Village, 1776

RIP AND WOLF BEGAN the easy descent toward the village which lay on the west bank of the Hudson and directly across from Tarrytown. Many of the modest wooden homes had been replaced by houses and farms built of small yellow bricks brought over from Holland with their latticed windows and gabled fronts and of course, the ubiquitous weathercock.

Soon they came upon the village inn displaying a colorful sign with the likeness of His Majesty George the Third. Most locals simply called it "The George." It being an exceptionally mild fall evening the innkeeper, Nicholas Vedder, held court outside where tables and chairs were set up under an enormous sycamore tree. The familiar faces of his patrons appeared stoic as they gathered around him, somberly smoking their clay pipes. The mood was especially gloomy that evening as the schoolmaster, Derrick Van Brummel, was summarizing the contents of a rare newspaper he had obtained and consoling his audience over the alarming subject matter with mutters of "tic-tic-tic" and several "well now's" accompanying the news briefing.

"Looks like Newburyport is a powder keg," said the lugubrious Van Brummel. "The alarm was raised that English troops marched out to make an attack at Lexington and Concord. Blood was spilled, mostly on the British side."

The news continued to be disturbing. "Oh, and it would seem that recently Le Chevalier de La Luzerne, the ambassador from the Court of Versaille, marched through Fish Kill on his way to Philadelphia to meet with General Washington with a troop of light dragoons."

"And this," he concluded the news summary. "There is the story of five British deserters who reported to officials in Pittsburgh that British troops were preparing to march south to Savanah. But a mutiny disrupted their plans which erupted over the failure of the English commander to provide the men their allowance of rum."

Once all the hand wringing and sighs were out, Peter Van Dam, by his having once attended a lecture at Harvard College, was trusted with the commentary by mutual consent of the gathering.

"Pity the British," he opined. "But even so, the people of Lexington and Concord will make them rue the day they spilled American blood. Taxes without a say, rubbish! This all could have been avoided. But bear me out, the colonies cannot stand against the might of the British and their allies. Even now they are courting the Onondagas, Cayugas, Senecas, and Mohawks and rousing them to make war on the rebels."

Van Dam continued, "And don't ye doubt the French are in this for profit. Mind you, I don't get between the French and British in their squabble over Ohio, that's none of our concern. But the French will not soon forget the French and Indian War, nor will Washington fail to recall his embarrassment with the fiasco at Fort Necessity after the battle of Jumonville Glenn in '54."

Van Dam wasn't finished and made his final comment on the third frightening report. "I say this about the South and their plantations. God will surely see to it that the South collapses with the British invasion because of their demonic enslavement of the Africans with no measure of mercy nor of earned freedom at all. People common as property. It's a doomed industry and not of man's invention but the Devil."

All heads, however, ultimately turned to Nicholas Vedder whose position as keeper of the inn and seller of a prized beer called Old Delft guaranteed him the final word, or rather the final puff. For when the commentary pleased him he would draw deeply on his pipe and emit tranquil columns of smoke. But when agitated he would huff and puff like a bellows, blowing angry black fumes into the air. Wordless but indisputable this constituted the final verdict for the assembly. That evening there was a dark cloud hovering over the gathering by the inn.

The village was neither a hotbed of rebel conspiracy nor a pillar of Tory support. Surely not as might be found among the Anglo-Americans. The fact was that the Dutch communities were generally complacent however, like the rest of the provinces, they could be divided into camps of rebels or patriots and Tories or Loyalists. If there were a slight edge toward the rebels in the Hudson Valley, it was because of Dutch antipathy for the British. Still, it made politics among the Knickerbockers awkward at best. Churches were emptied because of it, families divided, businesses closed, and each camp was wary and on the lookout for a cousin who might turn them in for a shilling or two.

The war placed the Dutch in a difficult bind. Their kind of patriotism was not of the English sort common among the Puritans and the generations that followed religious and secular. From the very beginning the colonists of rural New Netherland had a different reason for being in America. In broad terms, like the Dutch West India Company, the London establishment was intent on recreating the model of Caribbean plantations in America. America would simply be a colony to exploit, a network of plantations to ensure that as much wealth as possible be extracted from it. In contrast to the vagaries of the city of New Amsterdam as well as the schemes of the Dutch West India Company, the Dutch colonists of the rural villages and a host of Dutch intellectuals in New York, sought to recreate the Netherlands in America complete with churches, schools, privately owned businesses, universities, art galleries, concert halls, museums, and all that in their experience made civilization possible. Moreover, it was this progressive kind of Dutch tolerance that was exported to New Netherland. The colonists there were descended from people who were escaping war or economic deprivation and seeking a place of security for themselves and by reason of that, security for others. Also imported was the sense that free thinkers and creative minds should be welcomed. And while their model included economic success, it was not the exploitation and imperialism behind the plantation model.

That was precisely the thinking of the people of Rip Van Winkle's village, and Rip so desperately wished to join the assembly if just to enjoy the rounds of Old Delf, but he feared more the wrath of Katrina. He tarried a moment, but the prescient whining of Wolf reminded him that he carried their dinner in his game bag, and it was past time the stew be on the boil. Shortly man and dog turned from the main road out of the village to a craggy and overgrown path leading to a dilapidated farmhouse.

Weeds and brambles nearly covered the poorly maintained pathway of the ramshackle structure. Farm animals wandered in and out of broken fences. The ground was poorly tilled or untilled, and what grew was misshapen and besieged by insects, much of it rotting in the ground. The farmhouse roof was also in disrepair and seemed as if it would serve more as a sieve than a cover should it rain. The door to the house hung unevenly and the chimney, though producing smoke, was in bad need of repointing. All of it was in stark contrast to the other houses of the village which were in immaculate condition, swept and scrubbed in the Dutch fashion, with porches so clean they could easily have been outdoor patios.

No sooner had Rip and Wolf entered the house than the mistress began her tirade beginning with a brooming of old Wolf who skirted to his tiny corner of refuge in the kitchen. There, tail between his legs, twitching and shaking, he cowered before Katrina. Rip felt for his friend but for the time being, he welcomed his wife's attention turned elsewhere. Not for long. Finished with the dog Katrina began her rant reserved for Rip and would tolerate no interruptions. He could only recoil, but at the peak of her rage he held up his game bag and mumbled something like, "These need to be skinned and put in the pot for supper." He didn't wait for an answer but headed for the rundown shed behind the house where his rusty tools, knives, and hatchets were kept. Wolf darted after him glad to put some distance between him and the mistress.

Katrina's common sense was not in question as without her they probably would be homeless and destitute. She accepted the excuse by silently allowing Rip to butcher the meat. She put the pot on the fire and began scrubbing what few vegetables she was able to obtain from the market.

Dinner conversation was cold and seasonless much like the stew finally delivered. Katrina informed Rip that she had to go to town tomorrow as they were "out of everything," and she had managed to scrape together a few Spanish dollars. She ordered Rip to spend the day repairing the dilapidated fences with "no loafing, no sleeping, and no excuses."

When Rip woke the next morning she was gone. Relieved, he decided it was a perfect day for a hunting expedition in his beloved Catskill Mountains. He called to Wolf, shouldered his game bag and rifle, and together they set off for a day of pleasant loafing.

7

A Long Nap, 1776

IT WAS A SPLENDID autumn day, and Rip and Wolf wandered mindless of the path they chose. Their soft footsteps seemed reverently appropriate for the gentle breeze rustling through the forest creating a single note repeated each time the trees began to bend to its will. That was accompanied by songbirds, the cries of eagles, and the rustle of a small cataract. Occasionally the forest symphony was interrupted by Rip's rifle which would pierce the peace like a tympany roiling a lullaby. It was still early and yet he had two large squirrels in his bag.

Absentmindedly coming to a hilltop, he noticed that the forest trail had brought them to the highest eastern section of the stately Catskills. The climb had tuckered out both of them, and so Rip dropped his gun and game bag and fell breathlessly to the ground. But not before insuring it was not simply a convenient knoll, but one of deep soft grass where nearby grape vines ripe with fruit, berry bushes, and trees of various kinds would supply a snack and a picturesque view. From his reclining perch he could see for miles; the majestic Hudson adorned with the colorful sails of a three-masted warship; a second smaller vessel was a frigate; finally, there were two stealthy native canoes likely unnoticed by the ships. The clouds above reflected purple on the water. Rip was in his element, and it could only lead to a fine late-morning nap.

As he began to drift off to sleep he heard the distant cry of "halloo." He saw no one. Again, the "halloo," and this time the call of recognition. "You there, Van Winkle. Rip Van Winkle." He was never one to jump up from his repose except at the bark of Katrina, but this time he did so but saw no one. He scanned the forest around him and decided he had drifted off and was at the mercy of a dream. Wolf was unmoved which made the call suspicious anyway.

But there it was again, and this time Rip was wide awake as was Wolf who snarled while his hair stood on end. Rip was not confrontative in any manner, and Wolf was really a coward at heart. Both avoided trouble whenever possible, and Rip was more likely to run away or if asked, lend a hand. But this was no Indian. It was someone who knew his name and that unnerved him, especially as he expected no Europeans in these desolate woods unless it was a trapper. But the better game was down below and further west where the streams still produced abundant beavers and otters. No, this was not a hunter.

Fully awake and convinced it was no dream Rip felt a sense of foreboding. Still, the obscured figure of a man knew his name. Closer now he could make out the man's appearance. He was no more than four feet tall and wore a cloth jerkin tied with a leather belt around his waist. His pants were several layers of breeches the outer one being decorated with silver buttons along the side. His hair was long and white as snow as was his beard, but this was braided and studded with colorful beads. On his head he wore a conical hat not very tall, not like a dunce cap, but rather it was short and colored red. His manner was friendly, but his expression was serious. That might be explained by the considerable load he carried. It appeared from the shortening distance to be a keg most likely of beer nearly as tall as he.

Again the "halloo" rang out. "Give me a hand *jonge*." The familiar accent was clearly that of the Dutch Americans whose pronunciation of the old tongue was so changed it could not be mistaken by the locals nor understood by the people of the homeland. But here in the Hudson Valley it was a dialect familiar to everyone.

Always one to be of assistance Rip lifted the back end of the keg, and the two made their way down a deep ravine with Wolf tagging along behind. As they plodded on Rip could hear claps of thunder echoing off the walls of the ravine. Certain he would be drenched with rain he paused to pull up his collar nearly causing the keg to slip both their grasps. Still, they managed to hold tight, and before long Rip discovered the source of the resounding peals. There, in what was a naturally formed amphitheater, was a party of similarly dressed gnomish creatures. As for the thunder, it was the amplified sound of their bowling balls crashing against ninepins. Although clearly of the same clan, they could be distinguished for their dress and the outrageousness of their appearance. One seemed to be nothing more than a nose protruding from hat, hair, and beard. Another had a perfectly round head atop which was this time a tall conical hat adorned with feathers. In his belt was a fierce-looking cutlass. Two appeared to be brothers and twins. Dressed alike, their eyes were bugged out and sleepy looking. Their lips were so thin that with their bushy beards, you might doubt they had mouths. But what they all shared in common was Rip's traveling companion's serious manner. Several came up to him and bowed, but they neither smiled nor spoke. What conversation there was was directed by the largest and roundest of the party, who appeared in every way to be their leader. His tall, green cone hat was decorated with more than a dozen silver buttons and the long stem of his pipe came to rest on his enormous belly which served as a cradle. He was clearly the eldest and carried himself more regally than the others. It was also he that made the only effort to engage Rip. But that was no more than a "How do you do, I am Nicholas Van Totter, and you are Rip Van Winkle. We know you and your gentle ways."

Rip's traveling companion hoisted the keg on a raised flat rock, and now Rip realized that he was not only meant to help with the cargo but was to be their waiter. He was given several huge flagons which he carried to the solemn bowlers who received them without making eye contact nor speaking a word. After several rounds, the bowlers seemed content.

Unnoticed and with the party well supplied, Rip thought he might have a taste of the light brown liquid. Never in his life had he tasted a more heady, flavorful brew. Hops burst in his mouth, and the most delicious aroma filled his nostrils. The slightly sweet slightly bitter mix had magical quenching powers. There was no resisting the brew and after a third, he began to feel his head spinning. Soon he could no longer stand and after all, there was more than enough thick green grass to lie down on. Before long he fell into a deep sleep, deeper than even Rip Van Winkle could imagine.

When he awoke he was back where he had first met the keg-bearing traveler, the very same high hillock with its magnificent view and thick, soft grass. It was early morning and the sun had just come up. He first noticed his beard, that it was a yard longer. Then his gun which had rusted where it lay. The game bag was shredded and moldy, and the game was gone. His joints ached and it took several efforts even to stand.

"Surely I've slept more than a night and Katrina will have my head." It was then he noticed that Wolf was nowhere to be seen. That was exceedingly odd as the dog never left his side. He called out and then whistled but to no avail. Perhaps the bowlers had made off with his dog? He was determined to find out. So, he hoisted his now useless firearm and began the descent. But upon retracing the steps of the two-man one-dog keg caravan, he discovered the ravine was now a cataract, making any further progress impossible. He was hungry and although returning home left him with a supreme sense of dread, he convinced himself it was no good starving to death in the mountains.

The slog back to the village was painful. His stomach ached for food, his body for sore joints and muscles, and his mind was filled with trepidation over his wife's scolding for his mischief. But when he arrived at the outskirts of the village all that vanished in the sights and sounds he encountered. People, none of whom he knew, were dressed altogether differently. Their language was the same, but there were more English terms mixed in.

Not only were the people unfamiliar, but so were the houses. First of all, there were many more of them. Streets had been altered and the names on the houses and businesses were altogether new. He began to think that the magic of the mountains was playing tricks on him, as long had he believed that the Catskills harbored mystical creatures and supernatural powers. And then he came upon The George, a bit more rundown than he remembered, and yet with a newly painted sign which still bore the likeness of His Majesty George the Third. It seemed more brilliant now with a new coat of paint. The king's red coat was shining, his scepter shone brightly in one hand, and the gleaming crown upon his head was glittering. This helped to restore his sense of reality, and the general layout of the village, its proximity to the Hudson and its central roads, while strange, were clearly familiar. And there stood the old Sycamore, yet even larger than he remembered. All of it was just familiar enough for him to push his way through an encircling, inquisitive crowd of gawkers and taunters and march straight to his farmhouse. A few of the children followed hooting and clapping until they lost interest, and so he was alone again.

He found it with some difficulty so overgrown was the path, and the new buildings had him turned around. Anticipating the wrath of the mistress of the house, he slowed his pace and gathered himself as much as possible under the circumstances.

The house had completely gone to ruin, and it was hard to imagine anyone living there. Although a shrew, Katrina kept her indoors tidy and well-swept. Apparently no longer. He called out to the empty rooms amidst the dust and cobwebs but heard no reply. It was pointless to remain, so he decided to return to The George. It was a cool, early afternoon and the patrons were inside warming themselves by the fire and sipping Old Delft. The interior was changed and somewhat refurbished, but not substantially altered. He asked the unfamiliar barmaid for Nicholas Vedder and got a shock.

"Vedder," she almost shouted in astonishment, "Why he's been dead for eighteen years. How might ye be asking after Nicholas Vedder?"

"He was a friend," Rip muttered his lips trembling as tears welled up in his disbelieving eyes.

"What about Brom Dutcher?"

"He died in the war. Caught a cannonball at Stoney Point. Or so they say. Some claim he drowned at the crossing of the Delaware."

Rip sighed, "Ah, the war, we knew it was coming. Did the Americans prevail?"

"Shush, and don't speak of it at your peril. They were soundly put down. The British are in command of all of New England, and from Canada to Virginia and beyond. They have given we few Dutch of the Hudson Valley a free hand in most of our affairs, and we in turn pay the taxes they levy. Most of us work for the company."

"The company?" Rip had never heard of it.

"Are you daft, man, the British North America Company?" she snarled.

"What about the schoolmaster?"

"We have a schoolmaster, a very capable Englishman named Charles Hedge."

"No, I mean Derrick Van Brummel."

"Went to war too. Got killed at Bunker Hill."

"Pray tell, what is the year?"

"1796, don't ye know?"

Too shaken to ask about other friends, he enquired about the fate of Rip Van Winkle.

"He's there, standing by the great sycamore on the square."

Startled by that, Rip stepped out of the inn to take a look. Sure enough, there he was or his double. Not so long a beard and not so old, but it was his image. Ragged, standing up but leaning heavily on a staff, he seemed to be dosing. Rip could not doubt it was he and yet another he. He looked again, and the man in the ragged clothes and a hat with its brim turned up seemed to come to and asked why he stared and demanded to know his name.

Doubting his sanity, Rip did not answer. He went back into the inn and began to ramble on that he was not himself, but that was him over by the tree. That he had fallen asleep and lost his dog. That his gun had rusted and that he was bewitched and forlorn that everyone he knew, including himself, was gone. That he had apparently slept for twenty years.

Back in the inn the patrons had heard enough and traded shock for incredulity, winking and smiling. They all chuckled at the crazy story. But two of them were concerned about the possibility of the old fool becoming unhinged and causing trouble. The younger Rip was curious and went to the window to listen to the old man's rant. Overhearing the conspiracy of the two patrons, the younger Rip simply disappeared into the woods. The father sought to follow and ask more of him, but the young man was gone.

Outside, word got out as it always did in small villages, and a crowd had gathered. A young and attractive woman with a baby pushed through the mob. Being jostled the baby began to moan, but his mother calmed him saying, "Be still Rip, it's all right."

Hearing her voice and seeing her face, Rip asked her name.

"Judith Cardenier," she answered.

"No, your maiden name," Rip pleaded.

"Van Winkle. That was my pathetic brother you saw disappear into the woods, and we are Rip and Katrina Van Winkle's children. The sad story is my father went hunting in the mountains some twenty years ago and never returned. I was a small child when he went missing. After that he and his dog, Wolf, were never seen again, and we never learned if my father was killed by the Indians or suffered from a fatal accident."

"And your mother?" Rip stuttered.

"Dead. Seemed to have burst the vessels of her heart fuming at a crooked peddler she believed had swindled her."

Feeling somehow freed if unhinged by this news he could no longer contain himself and embraced her crying out that he was her father. "I am Rip Van Winkle returned from some mysterious spell of the mountains." Then turning to the crowd he said, "Don't you all know me?" And then to his daughter, "Look into my eyes and tell me who I am."

Judith looked away and then turned back to him. She stared deeply into his eyes and exclaimed, "Father? Is it you?" An old woman who had snaked through the crowd now approach Rip and sized him up and down. "'Tis him I declare it. I knew him well enough, and I tell you this is Rip Van Winkle." And then turning to Rip she said, "Ye must tell us where ye been."

At that, all who could fit into the inn with others standing at the open windows, followed Rip in and heard the strangest of all tales, about an encounter with the little people of the mountains, of the beer caravan, of the bowling party, of the bewitching brew that brought on a terrible sleep, and of his return home some twenty years later.

Satisfied that this was truly Rip Van Winkle, the patrons simply and quietly turned to the more immediate news of the British exploration and conquest of the lands to the west. Rip was given a home with Judith and her husband, and each day he who was no less lazy and no less prone to wander about his now more crowded mountains, would tell his story at the inn to any and all who had not yet heard it or who had heard it more than a dozen times but wanted to hear it again in exchange for beer and the details of the war.

8

The Revolt of the Colonies, 1796

To THAT END, EVERY day that Rip Van Winkle wasn't trudging through the Catskills he was telling his mysterious story in the inn. After settling in with Judith and with his first visit back to The George, he begged for news about the war. He remembered hearing about the battle of Lexington and Concord and pleaded with the patrons that they begin there. On this particular evening, he found company with two brothers, Smith by name, from Boston on their way to York, Pennsylvania, after an anticipated short stay with relatives in Paramus, New Jersey. They made it clear they were devoted Tories from the beginning. Rip noticed with some consternation that the number of British Loyalists had at least doubled since his encounter in the mountains. "Suddenly everyone's a Loyalist," he silently mused to himself.

The brothers had a room for the night and planned to be on their way first thing in the morning. With time to kill they ate a hearty dinner and settled by the fire, ordering port and cheese. Having heard Rip's incredible tale they were inclined to seek other company, but the inn's regulars swore by Rip's account, and so adamant were they that they convinced the gentlemen from Boston that it was all true. That settled, Rip asked again about the events at Lexington and Concord.

The older brother was Gavin Smith, and he took the lead accepting the fact that Rip was likely the only adult in British North America that did not know of the famous battle that initiated the violence of the rebellion. He reported that the redcoats had been in Boston since 1768 supported by a naval force and marines because of the trouble stirred up by the retaliatory British laws enacted after the Boston Tea Party.

"That I'm familiar with," Rip interrupted with a chuckle. "Imagine those Yankees dressed up like Indians. I'd have spotted the imposters in a second."

Gavin went on. "The laws essentially curtailed any right to self-government which instead of deterring the rebels, led to their forming the First Continental Congress to initiate protests and seek a way to respond to Great Britain's perfectly legal actions."

"That too I remember," Rip put in.

"Then you must remember all the ragged American colonial militias formed to defend against Indian attacks."

"I do, indeed," said Rip.

"Well, these became the genesis of the rebel army. It was around that time that the colonists who were advocating for freedom from Great Britain began calling themselves Americans. In 1774 they petitioned King George III threatening to boycott all British goods. That resulted in Great Britain declaring the Thirteen Colonies to be in rebellion. The Brits were determined to dispose of them, considering them nothing but disloyal rebels. It turned out that General Thomas Gage, the interim governor of Boston, had orders direct from London to put them down soundly. They had on hand about three thousand troops and were confident they could subdue the insurrection easily."

Gavin was quite animated now, "You see, Gage had gotten word that the rebels were trying to raise an army of about eighteen thousand men. To counter this initiative on the part of the new congress, Gage sent out a patrol on horseback to try and intercept any messages that were being delivered by the rebels. Of course, this gave the Continentals forewarning of an increased chance of a British attack."

The younger brother, John Smith, ordered a round of Old Delft for them and Gavin continued. "It was the morning of April 18, and I remember it well. Forewarned, the Lexington militia began to muster. That afternoon Gage gave the orders, and about seven hundred British regulars under Lieutenant Colonel Francis Smith marched from Boston to Concord. They were to seize and destroy any military stores they found. But instead of surprising the Yanks, no thanks to the traitors, Revere and Prescott, word went out. Churches like Old North in Boston signaled the alarm with lanterns in their steeples."

"Revere and Prescott?" Rip didn't know the names.

"Oh, my word, of course, you were having a nap. Paul Revere, Samuel Prescot, and some others went on horseback and successfully warned of the approach of the raiding party. This put the militias at the ready. Come sunup the battle at Lexington commenced. The Brits drew first blood and eight colonials died with only one regular perishing. The militia was outgunned and outmanned, so they retreated and broke apart once they reached Concord, about seven miles due west. They regrouped at North Bridge and overwhelmed a group of regulars by outnumbering them four to one. That forced them to fall back and regroup with the rest of their army. Then they began their march back to Boston being harassed every step of the way, but they did manage to make it to Charlestown albeit with significant casualties. Blocking the narrow access to the city, the regulars were able to hold off the rebels at the Siege of Boston."

"You know, the rebel army didn't even have a name." This time it was John who took over the narrative. "Washington called them the Troops of the United Provinces of North America, but the British simply referred to them as a 'rabble in arms.' It was all over the newspapers, saying how the British considered the rebels a disorderly mess. But Bunker Hill convinced them they had a fight on their hands."

"Yes, Bunker Hill. I've heard it was an important battle, but I know nothing of it nor of its outcome." Rip was hungry for more news of the war.

"Well," John took the lead, "it all began with that siege my brother spoke of. Boston is entered by a narrow strip of land almost making it more of an island than a peninsula. For the rebels, it meant keeping the British in Boston, but for the redcoats, it meant keeping the militias out. At the outset, the Americans outnumbered the British two to one. To the North, the British held Charlestown a great strategic advantage, and Beacon Hill was where the British had their headquarters. But the problem for the rebels from day one was that a siege of this magnitude required cannon and gunpowder both of which Washington had little of. Nor were his weapons of any decent quality. Their arms were humble, mostly fowling pieces and muskets. Unlike the British, few of them were armed with flintlocks. The rabble didn't even have uniforms. But by midsummer troops outside of New England began to show up. Some were woodsmen and marksmen. Their revolutionary riffled long barrels were accurate far beyond the musket, and they could hit a target at twice or more the distance of the musket. But mostly, the militias worked on building the needed ramparts."

"Don't forget about the raids," Gavin interjected.

"Right," replied John. "All this time both armies were conducting forays into the other's positions."

"Oh, and the bombardment," again it was Gavin.

"Indeed, the cannonade could go on for hours against the rebel positions," John agreed. "But it was a standoff. The month following Lexington and Concord, the Brits had been receiving new troops. They wanted to reinforce Bunker Hill and Dorchester Heights and secure the high ground there."

"About middle June the rebels were building redoubts on Bunker Hill and the British were intent on attacking them. The assaults were vicious, and many redcoats died. On the third try the Brits succeeded as the defenders simply ran out of ammunition. They had the Hill but at a great price."

"And so, the standoff at the siege of Boston continued. By late summer morale on both sides had collapsed. Disease was rampant. Food was in short supply."

John burst in. "They tore our ancestral home down for firewood. We lost everything, but we knew it was the fault of the cursed rebels."

Gavin got them back on track. "On both sides, but especially for the Brits, the most pressing need was for food. More time passed, the seasons changed, and with the threat of oncoming winter the siege was collapsing."

Gavin couldn't remain silent. "It was late November when the British evacuated the city of many of the sick, the women, and the children. Still, they dug in periodically receiving reinforcements. Meanwhile, they turned their attention to New York."

John interrupted. "We had our strongest loyalist support there except for New Jersey."

Gavin shushed him. "And the Brits whipped Arnold at Quebec."

"Arnold?" Rip was vaguely familiar with the name.

"Right! Benedict Arnold, hero of the war over North America, a favorite of His Majesty King George, and now governor of New York. But things might have been different if Colonel Henry Knox had succeeded in bringing the guns of Fort Ticonderoga down to Washington in Boston."

"Under Knox, the rebels planned to transport the guns by ship over Lake George which was as yet not frozen over. At the southern end was Fort George where they were held up by a tremendous thaw setting the convoy back several days. But a blizzard froze the lake, and they pushed on by sled to Albany. Knox planned to cut holes in the frozen Hudson which would serve to strengthen the ice. But as he and a few others were making their way to the river a British marksman killed Knox."

John the more dramatic brother added, "Shot him right through the head. They say he was dead before he hit the ground. That put an end to the plan to strengthen the ice. It proved to be a grave mistake."

Gavin took over. "Mistake it was. News that came days later was that General Schuyler wrote to Washington that halfway across the river the ice gave way to the loss of all but one sled of cannon, and most of the supporting militia and teamsters perished in the icy water. The brilliant plan to bring artillery to Washington ended in disaster and was abandoned."

Rip opined, "Alas, it was a foolhardy scheme to begin with, fraught with bad luck and bad weather. But I have been told things went better for the Yankees at Dorchester. What can you tell me about that battle?"

"Well," John complied, "as important an event as Dorchester was it was hardly a battle. It might have been but again for the weather. Washington was through with waiting and determined to take Dorchester. He brought up what few guns had survived the Albany disaster and secretly built fortifications at Dorchester. The general had nearly nine thousand men at his disposal. On March 5th the assault on Boston began with the cannon fire lasting through the night. The British retaliated, but neither side did much damage. On the third night with the first blast of cannon fire, the American, General John Thomas, led his men to the Dorchester shores."

Gavin interrupted, "But thanks to the quick thinking of General Francis Smith, who having gotten word of the rebel advance, immediately rallied his troops to meet them."

"Right," agreed John, "and for good reason. Although the work done on the fortifications was momentous, our boys were now prepared. Still, the high ground was occupied by the rebels, and it made an all-out assault the only option. General Howe who commanded the British army was determined to take Dorchester Heights. And then the weather intervened. The painful experience at Bunker Hill and a massive storm convinced Howe that an assault was out of the question. But time was running out, supplies running short, and in spite of spoiling for a fight, Howe ordered the withdrawal of his troops and the few remaining Loyalists from Boston. Boston lay in ruin but now unoccupied, and so the British focus turned to York Island the renamed island of the old Indian name *Mannahata*."

"Ah, now you're getting to my neck of the woods. Never did I understand the ways of you New Englanders with all your internal bickering." Rip had grown up with the Knickerbockers' hostility toward New England. Equally, the Dutch harbored great annoyance with the British insofar as they were frequently at war, and it was natural that the Knickerbockers felt similarly in America. "So, tell me about York Island then," Rip begged the brothers.

"Well," said Gavin, "the British set sail for New York, and the rebels marched to intercept them all the time knowing that York Island was not Boston. The island's geography meant that it would be at the mercy of the better navy, and the British Navy was and is the best in the world. Moreover, New York was packed with Loyalists, and the vast majority of Dutch farmers on Long Island were on the side of the British as well. But as for the city, with word out about the British advance most had evacuated to the country."

"The first of the British fleet arrived at the end of June. In short order, at least forty-five British ships were anchored near Sandy Hook, in New Jersey. Meanwhile, in Philadelphia, the rebel congress had officially declared its independence from Great Britain. In early July two of His Majesty's ships sailed into New York Harbor. Old Fort George opened fire with the British ships returning fire. But their mission was to proceed ahead and cut off any support that might come from the rebels up north. In mid-July Howe sent a delegation to ask for Washington's surrender which he refused to do. All the while British ship after ship arrived in New York Harbor. One, the HMS *Victory*, mounted 98 guns."

John couldn't hold his tongue any longer knowing the war was coming down to several pivotal battles. "The long-anticipated invasion of Long Island, now called the Battle of Brooklyn, began on August 22, with several British frigates and bomb ketches anchored in the Narrows separating Brooklyn from Staten Island. They would cover the landing. At daybreak, a large contingent of troops on flatboats pushed off and quickly offloaded their troops at Gravesend Bay south of York City. Many of your Dutch Loyalists greeted the troops and made provision for them."

"Me, a Loyalist?" ventured Rip. "I took no side one way or the other. Not my fight."

Gavin wasn't pleased with Rip's complacency. "Well, you had better be deciding or you might find yourself in hot water."

"Who would bother with an old Knickerbocker like me? Anyway, on with your story."

Gavin was fuming so John took over. "The key to British success was an overlooked narrows called Jamaica Pass. Leadership for the attack was handed over to General Henry Clinton who had distinguished himself in the victory over the rebels at Fort Sullivan in Charleston. At Fort Sullivan he overcame his initial reluctance to risk his troops, and indeed crossing over to the north end of Sullivan's Island lost him many a good man. But after two sloops of war supported his advance and demonstrating a great deal of courage, Clinton captured the fort and accepted the surrender of Colonel Moultrie. That battle convinced him that the war should be conducted by outflanking the enemy rather than by seeking to conquer territory. He was able to convince General Howe of the successful strategy."

Gavin decided he was the better historian. "With General Grant and the Hessian mercenaries under General von Heister creating a diversion, Clinton and then Howe behind him made their way through Jamaica Pass. The commencing of the diversion began with British guns opening fire near Gowanus Bay to the southwest and the Hessian guns joined by Cornwallis at Flatbush further east. It appeared a standoff until suddenly, out of nowhere, Clinton's men followed by Howe and his army came at the rebels from behind. The Yanks were completely surrounded. The Yankee general John Sullivan was captured, and the rebels ran for their lives."

Gavin had picked up the pace and his voice rose an octave. "Howe was advised by Clinton to press on, which he did with all the fury the British and Hessian armies could muster. But once again the weather intervened. Although severely slowed by the storm, the Redcoats and mercenaries had nothing else to prevent their advance and in spite of a slog through mud and a driving wind that nearly blinded them, they took Fort Box and Fort Greene capturing hundreds of rebel soldiers."

"Meanwhile Washington was making plans for an evacuation of Brooklyn to New York but unless a miracle were to transpire, he knew there would not be time. However, as was so often the case, the weather intervened with an intensifying storm, and the British were stopped with all operations halted. Storm or not the Yanks' desperation forced them to risk everything. From New York flatboats were able to approach where the Brooklyn Ferry operated, and when the storm let up just enough, Washington led what remained of his troops to the boats. A terrible tide and wind kept the British ships from getting around Governors Island otherwise the war would have been over. Nevertheless, Howe ordered the ground attack at the backs of the retreating rebels. Rather than fight, Washington decided to save as many men and arms as he could. He ordered a line of soldiers to stop the advancing Redcoats knowing full well they would pay with their lives. The bloodbath was gruesome as the rear guard became fodder to save the others. It was estimated only four thousand of the nearly ten thousand rebels made it safely to New York."

Gavin was nearly breathless at this point but continued. "By September British ships and flatboats full of troops were heading up the East River toward Kips Bay. Howe delivered a peace overture that was rejected by Washington. In response, Howe let loose a terrific barrage that pulverized the island's parapets. Of course, the Yanks fled making their way to New York and then out of the city north. It was a rout and soon the British were in full control of New York as the Loyalists poured out into the streets to celebrate the victory." Gavin went quiet utterly out of breath.

John stepped in. "But in their haste to finish off the rebels they were met by a force of woodsmen who managed to turn the redcoats around in retreat. Meanwhile, a fire decimated the city. They blamed Captain Nathan Hale for the fire, accused him of being a spy, and summarily hanged him."

Gavin was still catching his breath. "On October 17 Washington ordered the evacuation of York Island, and the British chased them to White Plains with skirmish after skirmish. On the high ground of Chatterton Hill Washington gave orders to return fire with the few cannons he had. It was enough to slow the British. But then inexplicably the British force turned and headed southwest towards the Hudson. Many on both sides speculated they were going for Fort Washington. It was indeed the case, and there the Hessians proved their mettle. It was mid-November when the rebel colonel, Robert Magaw, surrendered."

Having recovered and fortified by another mug of Old Delft, Gavin insisted on taking over. "Abandoning Fort Lee by late November Washington and his troops were in full retreat across New Jersey knowing full well that of all the colonies Loyalist support in New Jersey was the greatest. The Redcoats and Hessian mercenaries chased them to Newark only to find it abandoned with the rebels now well on their way to the Brunswicks. Without guns and soldiers, it was impossible to hold the Brunswicks, and so Washington made haste for Trenton. Indeed, thousands came out to welcome the British. Exhausted, the troops left off their pursuit and rested. But once Howe arrived in New Brunswick in early December he ordered the troops to resume the chase."

Gavin went on. "When Washington got news of this he decided to move his worn-out troops across the Delaware to Pennsylvania. Meanwhile, the British had accomplished another coup with the capture of Washington's second in command, the formidable General Lee. Still, with the rebels in his sights, Howe decided to curtail any offensive until spring with the cold weather setting in."

"The Congress must have reasoned that in time Howe would seek to take Philadelphia, and they moved their headquarters to Baltimore. Severely stung but far from dead, the rebels planned to retake Trenton. Christmas night Washington's troops crossed the Delaware and at eight in the morning through blinding snow, they began their surprise attack. Gaining the town the Redcoats and Hessians engaged in hand-to-hand combat with the rebels. Surprised and surrounded the Hessians surrendered. After securing the weapons and stores the rebels returned to the Pennsylvania side of the Delaware. The small victory immediately raised the prospects for the rebels at large, and Washington decided on a strategy of surprise attacks and withdrawals. The Yanks scored another victory just outside of Princeton. And now, thanks to a number of American victories, the spineless French began offering support until the tide turned again and French naval support evaporated. As such, it was as if things were at a draw, and the next several battles would be decisive shifting the balance of power one way or another. That pivotal battle was the battle of Bennington."

"John studied that battle very carefully and knows it better than I," said Gavin and John continued. "Under General John Bergoyne a colorful assortment of soldiers and Indians were intent on securing Albany under British control. Rebel attempts to raise an army failed and perfect weather allowed the Hessians to advance, but they were too widely dispersed. Their leader, Lieutenant Colonel Friedrich Baum, immediately ordered them to support the redoubt Baum had raised. Meanwhile, the march of a contingent of the Green Mountain boys ended in disaster when they were ambushed by a large force of Canadians and Indians who surprised them, killed many, and sent the rest running for their lives back to Vermont. Holding the hill and preparing for a dangerous assault on the rebels the British were suddenly reinforced by Lieutenant Colonel Heinrich von Breymann, who personally led the charge on the rebel forces. The loss served to reverse the optimism that had been generated by the previous victories, and it left Bergoyne free to march on Albany."

"Gavin knows the war's conclusion better than I do," said John, as he turned his attention to his newly filled mug.

"Right you are," replied Gavin and he began. "Bergoyne reached Saratoga mid-September. Morale among his troops was at a high point having defeated a superior army under the leadership of General Gates at the battle of Freeman Farms. Bergoyne planned on flanking the rebels but under the command of Benedict Arnold, the rebels had other ideas. However, Arnold may have already doubted where his loyalties lay and did nothing to stop Bergoyne who overran his troops. Arnold managed to escape along with a large part of his army. But the day belonged to the British and to Bergoyne. This meant that the British Northern Strategy had succeeded as Bergoyne went on to capture Albany."

"Meanwhile in August Howe realized his ambition to march on Philadelphia. It proceeded in early September with the Battle of Brandywine. Washington committed a serious error in leaving his right flank open and Howe's wing broke through with Lieutenant General Wilhelm von Knyphausen attacking the rebel's left wing. That left Philadelphia vulnerable, and in two weeks' time the city was taken. Howe got his trophy."

It was still in Gavin's hands. "In July 1779, the rebels attempted to take Stony Point and Paulus Hook but were defeated by Howe's troops. Things were at a bit of a standstill, but one year later Howe's troops with a large contingent of Hessians retook New Jersey at the Battle of Connecticut Farms. Moving out from Elizabethtown Brigadier General William Maxwell and his New Jersey Brigade tried to halt the Hessian advance using the Fabian strategy of deception, poking, and prodding the enemy. But by now the tactics had become familiar to both sides, and the Hessians employed them equally well. They drove the rebels back and reengaged them at the Battle of Springfield. Outflanked by the Queen's Rangers the farm was soon in British hands."

"That same month the illustrious former commander of West Point, Benedict Arnold, proved his loyalty to the king by joining Howe's forces and providing vital intelligence through his agent John André. He was immediately promoted to Lieutenant General and put in charge of Washington's capture. But the southern strategy had dragged on and became a kind of stalemate with the armies trading victories and defeats. This, however, led to the pivotal Battle over Yorktown. Without French naval support on August 31, fortified and benefitting from perfect weather conditions, the British Admiral Graves was able to reinforce Cornwallis at Yorktown. Anticipating an attack on Yorktown, Washington marched out of Williamsburg to surround Yorktown. His assault began with a heavy bombardment of the city after which they closed in. It was then that without the rebels' knowledge, Cornwallis received five thousand soldiers in relief. After repelling several frontal assaults, the rebels dug in. Washington made a trip to the front lines in order to plan his best strategy. The final visit to the front proved disastrous as it coincided with a flanking maneuver by the reinforced British to dislodge the nearest rebel emplacements. Surprised and realizing his mistake, Washington attempted a diversionary tactic but failed, and he and his party were captured with many rebels killed. With Washington on his way to New York in chains the rebel forces collapsed and most deserted to their homes throughout the colonies. Howe arrived days later to finish the job."

Gavin concluded the story. "With the capture of Washington, the French withdrew all their support. Alexander Hamilton surrendered to General Howe on October 14, 1781. Washington was sent to England where he was tried and hanged for treason. Most of the leaders of the rebellion were hunted down, some recanted and were spared, and many others were caught and hanged or shot trying to escape. The Continental Congress collapsed. One by one the northern and southern colonies surrendered, and in 1783 the British began their full occupation of British North America, which would include all of the territory below Canada and to the south and west as far as the border with Mexico."

Heads were nodding off and even the storytellers were fading fast. It was late and long past the hour of closing. The fire had died out and the inn was becoming cold. Gert De Jong had joined the small audience content to listen to this riveting account of the war, but now she was closing up. The members of the party were off to bed, and Rip was eagerly anticipating a long sleep through the morning. The obliging Smith brothers were pleased to have entertained the group, but they too were eager for bed as they had a long trip to make the next day.

9

British North America, 1783

FOLLOWING THEIR SUCCESSFUL DEFEAT of the rebels, British rule was solidified in North America. From the border of Canada south to the tip of Florida, from York Island west to the Pacific Ocean, these vast areas became known to the world as British North America. It seemed astonishing to some that the newly acquired territory was forty times the size of the United Kingdom. Nevertheless, his Majesty King George III was sovereign over the largest and soon-to-be richest empire in the world.

George had become king of Great Britain in 1760 with the death of his father, George II, and ruled with a constitutional monarchy, which meant that George shared power through his ministerial government with the British Parliament. However, his rule was severely weakened by the costly Seven Years' War with France, and a rift created by his favoring the Tories over the Whigs. But with the end of the war with France and the signing of the Peace of Paris Agreement in 1763, things began to look up for George and Great Britain.

Far beyond anything else, it was his armies' success over the troops of Washington that secured his undisputed rule over Great Britain, along with the wealth and prestige it brought him. In London the formerly influential groups who sympathized with the rebel cause lost their leverage and were swept away, most of them

Whigs. And some who had been too vehement in their criticism of George and the war wound up in the tower of London, including the Marquess of Rockingham and Edmund Burke. The Whig Party withered to the point that the ministry and the Tory Party ruled England with the crown for the astonishing next seventy-nine years. Great Britain had become in essence an oligarchy. Their grip on power would only strengthen with the continued success of the old British East India Company (1600) and the immediate success of the newly formed British North America Company. Never in the history of the world had global commercial companies wielded such power.

But it was not growing wealth alone that raised the prospects of George's rule. Part of his increasing success was his improved diplomatic skills. Throughout the seventeenth century and into the eighteenth century, Parliament passed laws that restricted the rights and freedoms of non-Anglican traditions. Catholics and Dissenters were not allowed to hold public office. This was especially the position of the Tory Party, while Whigs were typically the defenders of toleration, individual rights, and political reforms. The Tories, on the other hand, supported the power of the king and opposed reforms. But although Great Britain was now secure in its established Anglicanism, George compelled Parliament to revoke the Toleration Act of 1689 without much resistance. Recognizing the inevitable he had them relax many of the previously harsh restrictions on the public worship of other faiths. Sympathetic to Roman Catholicism he restored their civil rights, and some Protestant groups were allowed to worship freely. Nevertheless, those of the so-called Radical Reformation including Baptists and Quakers were outlawed, and they continued to be persecuted.

The Whigs were floundering and desperately sought a platform that would return them to power. They had the support of the dissenting groups and pressed the companies for reforms especially religiously speaking, such that they would sponsor missionary efforts throughout the world. The near collapse of the Whig Party curtailed any hope of major reforms, and Whig aspirations were worse than ever.

In British North America the newly appointed governor-general of the only Baptist colony in Rhode Island, Marion Wells, severely curbed Baptist worship and instituted legal measures to make their lives virtually intolerable. In some measure, it was payback for the colony's early declaration of independence from Great Britain on May 4, 1776, and their attack on the British warship the HMS Gaspee. But also, George considered the Baptists heretics and their notion of religious toleration abominable. Understandably then, the city of Newport, a Loyalist stronghold, replaced Providence as the provincial capital and headquarters of the governor-general and the British North America Company. With that, the increasingly popular idea of tolerance pioneered by the colony's founder, Roger Williams, was crushed for the time being.

As for Quaker Pennsylvania, the Friends were pacifists and stayed out of the war. For that they were tolerated and rewarded by being left alone. Also, owing to the fact that the Quaker, William Penn, had received his land grant from the English crown, there was sentiment in England that Pennsylvania was fairly gotten. However, self-rule was out of the question, and governance of the province was turned over to the British who allowed for both Quaker and Presbyterian worship. This pacified the Presbyterians, especially the Scots Irish, who had been arriving in great numbers to the colonies of North America, especially Pennsylvania, since 1710. As many as 200,000 Scots and Scots Irish emigrated before 1775. The British rulers simply saw them as cheap labor for the government-controlled and company-operated farms and plantations. After the war, the flow increased, but neither Quaker nor Presbyterian local rule was allowed. All of British North America was established Anglican, and the provinces of the territory were in the hands of British-appointed governors-general most of whom were from prominent families in England continuing the long-standing practice of patronage by the British companies. They were carefully vetted, loyal to the crown, and paid for and overseen by the British North America Company.

Necessarily, after the war, the King focused on restoring economic growth. The largest measurable downside of the war, besides the loss of human life, was the cost and incurred debt. The price tag of the war to the British was an estimated 240 million pounds. Yet by the time Great Britain went to war again with France in 1793, it was wealthier and more powerful than it had ever been. A great deal of that was due to the productivity of both the British East India Company and the British North America Company.

Immediately, George embraced the pre-war plantation model for the American colonies based on the success of the British East India Company, and it was clear the investors in the British North America Company would follow suit. As a result, nothing much changed in the South for the beleaguered African Americans. In fact, slavery accelerated at an alarming rate as Indigenous plantation owners were augmented by a growing number of new arrivals put there by the newly founded British North America Company, again created on the model of the East India Company. Plantations previously owned and operated by the Southerners were allowed to continue operation but were heavily taxed and overseen by the company. Each year they were required to reapply to the company for a license to operate. Initially this was met with hostility in the South, but most of the plantations were now in the hands of Loyalists, and they recognized where their interests lie. Southern patriotism evaporated in the war's aftermath. If there was lingering hostility it was kept secret except among the old, landed Southern families.

In Great Britain, the Quakers had been agitating to abolish slavery for years. But the greediest of the businessmen harbored no doubt that George was unsympathetic to Quaker reforms. Still, many in Great Britain were pressing hard for the end of slavery on what was initially a moral agenda. The sentiment never gained momentum until it began to appear to the London-based businessmen that the international slave trade, both pre-and post-war, among the Dutch, Spanish, French, Portuguese, and Southern colonies of North America, led to growing unprofitability. It produced so much competition that the idea emerged that perhaps the Quaker initiative might be a wise strategic move. By pulling the plug on slavery they could weaken their rivals while appearing to be the empire that took the moral high ground. But with the success of the war against Washington and the Continental Congress, the sheer magnitude of wealth being generated for Great Britain by colonialism and the British monopoly in slave trade in North America dashed any hope that the abominable trade in human beings would be abolished. The global commerce to London in slaves overseen by the British East India Company and now the newly formed British North America Company, was simply too lucrative to be defeated by a moral imperative. It was decided that if Great Britain was to capitalize on ownership of the southern territories it would have to maintain, indeed accelerate, the slave trade.

George III was well aware of that. He had, however, learned lessons from the history of the revolution, and his dealings with the Yankees were more measured. With a loose hand on the oversite of the British North America Company, he made popular concessions mostly on the question of religious practice. However, he solidified his unquestioned control of North America by restructuring the provinces such that he was able to create a British aristocracy deriving directly from family connections to the crown and the British North America Company. As a small concession, he found prominent positions for old Loyalists who grew wealthy as company leaders in the development and exploitation of British North America. Any objections from former rebels or Whigish reformers were met with either silence or the threat of punishment. The few violent outbreaks of protest, several initiated by the enslaved people, were swiftly thwarted. A single exception among the white population was a small cluster of Knickerbockers. The war hadn't changed life for most of the rural Dutch, but for a minority, especially in New York City, the war entirely changed their lives.

Of course, the outstanding hero of the war was Sir William Howe, and he was decorated and richly rewarded, retiring in luxury on an Irish estate given to him by the crown. Another hero, Benedict Arnold, was made governor-general of the Province of Massachusetts by George, but his life was cut short in 1785 when he was assassinated by a descendant of Nathan Hale, Jonathan Hale, who was summarily hanged. With most of the rebel leaders either dead, captured, or closely watched, the leadership of the cause of the Troops of the United Provinces of North America collapsed.

This meant that among the rural Dutch, life on the small farms of the Hudson Valley and the grander agrarian estates of Long Island and New Jersey, went on in resigned support of British rule. They didn't like the British, but they were a practical and essentially complacent people. However, on York Island, especially in New York City, a small number of Dutch patriots, former leaders of the city, still harbored a hatred of British rule and were devoted to the cause of freedom, self-rule, and the Dutch model for North America. They organized a clandestine, underground movement whose goal was to achieve independence from Great Britain. Hunted and frequently betrayed, around 1810 they developed the most sophisticated security network in the world deriving from the old Netherlands Polder Model of organization.

Polders were low-lying tracts of Dutch land surrounded by dykes, and they constituted the topography of the Netherlands as far back as the Middle Ages. The country was literally land reclaimed from the sea, and that required constant attention to the pumping stations that kept the sea out. Without the cooperation of everyone in and around the polder, the sea would reclaim the land. Consequently, even at times of conflict between the polders the Dutch cooperated with each other in order to maintain the pumps and dykes. This in time became characteristic of Dutch culture as the necessity to cooperate became essential to their survival. Cooperation even in times of hostility facilitated the way they were able to set aside differences for a greater purpose. This in turn required listening to the various parties and interests with the goal of slow but equitable decision-making. It became the model for Dutch rebellion in America.

However, the movement had little impact. It did manage to recruit a few of the most effectual and learned leaders of the failed rebel cause, those that were not dead or imprisoned. They in turn were bringing in small numbers of carefully vetted neophytes, sympathizers to the cause of freedom from Great Britain.

Meanwhile, British explorers were discovering just how enormous North America was. British ships had been active along the Pacific coast for years, but now that exploration intensified. Likewise, on land, with the help of the Indigenous and American-born Europeans and Africans, British exploration and lexicography exploded.

With very little deviation, the British North America Company plan followed the reasoning and structure of the British East India Company. However, although the South would be developed around large plantations, it became obvious soon enough that the plantation model was much less effective in the northern provinces. The climate and geography were simply wrong for the crops best suited for export back to Great Britain and elsewhere around the world, including tobacco, cotton, sugar, rice, and indigo. The same was true of the developing West. A plantation model was simply not feasible. Nor had they found large deposits of precious metals in the explored East as with Brazil, so mining was ineffectual. Still, there were productive plantations in Rhode Island, New Jersey, Long Island, and Pennsylvania, and they were built and worked by enslaved Africans. However, recognition that small farms were more efficient in the North led to an adjusted model which focused on agriculture to feed the South and the growing industrial complex of the North.

10

A Last Nap, 1803

WAKING FROM A GOOD night's sleep at his daughter's home, Rip Van Winkle yawned and rubbed his old and steadily failing eyes. It was late mid-morning, and his joints were stiff and sore under-standably so for a man in his seventies. His first thought was for a hike in his beloved Catskills, but on this particular morning he felt especially achy and decided instead to visit neighbors in town, after which he would join the patrons of The George for some sto-rytelling and Old Delft.

He dropped in on Hendrika Wind, the woman who first recognized him when he returned from his twenty-year sleep. The two reminisced about the days before his disappearance, and they shared memories of friends now long dead. When it came to Nicholas Vedder they both shed tears and joked and laughed at the brilliance of his pipe and the control he had over the smoke that billowed from it. She fed him a splendid lunch of soup, cheese, and bread, and from there he made his way to the town center where he was met by a small gaggle of children with their dogs playing the ancient Dutch game of *Spijkerpoepen* or Pooping Nails. The children took turns pinning strings tied at the end to a nail to the back of their knickers. Then they would move their hips in such a way as to try and drop the nail into a bottle placed on the ground. The children insisted old Rip have a go. He was considered a master at the game and before anyone could say Rip Van Winkle, he had the nail inside the bottle. Laughing and joyous he left them to their game as he made his way to The George.

The tavern was filled with smoke and familiar faces, all of whom smiled and shouted out their welcome to their most famous citizen. The patrons were in an especially jolly mood as a new shipment of Old Delft was recently delivered. It was brewed four weeks ago and so aged to perfection. Moreover, the cook, Betts Wallinga, had made a huge cauldron of savory venison stew seasoned with fresh herbs and spices, and braised in the new batch of Old Delft. For starters, the offering was a plate of pickled herring, and accompanying the stew was fresh baked Dutch Waldkorn Bread. To finish Betts had baked a dozen pies with fresh apples just ripe from the fall harvest.

Rip was still full from his lunch with Hendrika, but he could not resist indulging himself in a helping of all that was on offer. Contented and light-headed from the beer, he was dozing by the fire too tired to engage in more storytelling when a man spoke his name.

"Am I addressing the likes of Rip Van Winkle himself?" The stranger had to say it again to fully rouse Rip from his slumber. "Van Winkle is my name, and I am he," responded Rip who never failed to be friendly and engaging. "How might I help you?" the old rover asked.

"Is it true then, I am in the company of the legendary Rip Van Winkle, the most famous explorer of the mysterious Catskills, the teller of fabulous stories, and friend to all he meets?" The stranger was certainly flattering.

"Again, I tell you, I am he." Rip was clearly delighted to find he was such a celebrity when he himself had no idea that was the case. "And to whom do I have the pleasure of this conversation?" Rip was pleased and curious all at the same time."

"Shhh," was the stranger's reply. And then his deep blue eyes darted back and forth, surveying the room and lowering the brim of his hat so as not to be seen searching the premises. "Might you take me to a dark corner where we can drink and talk?"

"Drink and talk, you say?" Rip was a bit too loud but his enthusiasm for two of the things he enjoyed most in life got the better of him.

"Shhh," again was the caution. "Aye, to drink and talk, that is my intention upon meeting the most illustrious man of the valley."

"You are much too kind and yes, your offer is graciously received and warmly accepted. I know a corner where few can see and none can hear, but I know of no conspiracy nor treasure that might be hidden, nor do I involve myself in activities that might need discretion. In fact, you will find me a pinnacle of indiscretion." Rip's laugh was again too loud for the stranger.

"I beg you, Master Van Winkle, just a bit quieter, and off we go to your corner. I have some news to share with you, and it is of vital importance."

"Yes, of course, but first your name good sir."

"I am Lars Scholte from New York City. Let's be off to that corner of yours."

Rip took hold of his flagon and led the way to a dark corner of the inn. "Now what is it that brings you to our village and to me especially? And what is so urgent that it requires our privacy?"

"Master Van Winkle, what do you know of the polder?"

"Please, no more of this master business, and leave off my surname. Just plain Rip will do nicely. No, no polder. Never heard of it. Sounds Dutch though."

"Aye," replied Lars. "Dutch it is and Dutch it remains. But now it has become so much more. It is the name of a secret group of patriotic Americans, Dutch, Africans, Jews, British, and all who love liberty and dream of the day of American freedom from British rule."

"Are you mad man? Words like that can land you on the gallows?" Rip was never one to involve himself in politics, let alone rebellion against the government.

"Rip, I have come here by request of the polder to acquire your services."

Rip let out a laugh that startled even the drunkest patrons.

"Again sir, I must beg you to be quiet and discreet. Lives are at risk."

"Perhaps yours and yours alone, but not mine. I am an old man with nothing to offer rebels. I cannot fight. I have no head for politics. I do not enjoy the company of the elite, and I shun all forms of intrigue. My talent is in storytelling and hoisting a pint or two. And in my younger days, I could shoot the eye out of a squirrel at thirty yards. Perhaps you have the wrong Rip Van Winkle."

"No, it is you we seek, and aye we know of your habits, Rip Van Winkle, but it is your name and your support we are after, not your skill or knowledge. We want to count you among us for the encouragement and support it will lend our cause. We want to boast that Rip Van Winkle is among the polder, ready to assist in our rebellion."

"Sir, I do believe I am due home at this very moment. Now will you excuse me, please?"

"Just wait and hear me out. We are nearing the time that we will raise up arms against the British. Beginning with a few brave Knickerbockers we have built an underground resistance of significant formidability. Carrying on the dream of a country styled on the glory of the Netherlands and its enlightened humanism and reverence for God, we have silently lifted the flag of a new republic dedicated to the principles of tolerance and goodwill. The secure underground of the polder has strategically placed patriot leaders throughout the land. Every province is awaiting instructions. Men are at the ready, and arms and supplies have been stockpiled for years in preparation. Spies are as thick as flies in our cause. Our assassins await word. We have only months before the clarion call goes out and this country will be returned to its humane course. Slavery will be abolished, the evil British North American Company vanquished, the provinces brought into a confederacy, and the rights of men guaranteed by a constitution based on liberty, fraternity, equality, and human rights. The horrid institution of slavery will be abolished forever. Self-rule will be instituted with the pledge that each of the United Provinces of North America will be allowed to govern according to its historical colonial past with the exception of human exploitation, and united by an even-handed federal egalitarianism with a bill assuring the rights of every man, woman, and child. We are dedicated to detached decision making; to setting aside individual needs temporarily for the good of the whole."

Not pausing for a moment so as to be interrupted, Lars went on. "We have been assured by the patriotic leaders in the Western provinces and territories that we have their full support. As we speak Great Britain is at war with Mexico, which has severely curtailed her designs on the West Coast and Southwest. She is also battling the armies of Napoleon. She may be rich from her bleeding us dry, but she is distracted and stretched far beyond her limits."

Suddenly, there was a crash and a howl as mugs of beer went flying into the air. A string of curses from the mouth of Gert De Jong was aimed at the drunken lodger who stumbled into her as she served a table.

When Lars looked back Rip was gone. Slipped out without a sound in his most practiced manner. Lars shook his head, quaffed his last swallow of Old Delft, and dejectedly went to his room frustrated that he had failed in his secret mission. "Perhaps I will pay one more visit to Rip Van Winkle in the morning. I know he lodges with his daughter, Judith, and perhaps I can convince him of our cause." With that, he went to bed.

"Imagine the foolishness of such a scheme. And to think I would be a party to it. An old man like me." Rip was utterly undone. "If this gets out the company just might have at me. Best thing for me to do now is to spend tomorrow up in the mountains. Hopefully, that fool Lars will be on his way, and no one will be the wiser for it. But just in case, I will be off at first light."

It was indeed the case that Rip was distraught enough to rise, dress, find his squirreling rifle and game bag, and be off at dawn. When Lars Scholte came knocking at the door, Judith said he had missed his father who was up with the sun and off on a hunting trip in the mountains.

"The old dodger," Lars grumbled and with all his cards played, he had no choice but to dejectedly return to New York. However, now nothing would slow the momentum. Revolution was in the air.

Rip blessed his maker that it was a bright, wonderfully warm sunny fall morning. The warm air helped him stretch and move his aching joints enough to carry him out the door and off to a very special place he had fantasized about for years but dared not return to. It was the beautiful knoll where he had sought repose so many years ago with its majestic view of the river. He found the climb twice the ordeal of yesteryear, and huffing and puffing he threw himself down on the spot that he remembered in his nightmares.

No, he would not sleep nor venture even to close his eyes, but simply to rest briefly. This was all about the view, the berries, and giving Lars the slip. Anyway, he would not be staying long, and even now he was feeling hungry. He missed old Wolf more than ever, and he called his name. Contrary to his better judgment the physical exertion was such that he began to doze and then fell into a deep sleep.

"Your dog is with us," came a loud voice out of nowhere.

You could not say Rip Van Winkle jumped up from his slumber because he was no longer able to jump, or for that matter rise quickly. Although significantly startled, instead he crawled like a beetle sideways to a nearby rock, steadied himself, and pulled himself up eyes wide and panicked.

"What's all the fuss about old Rip, ye know me."

Rip Van Winkle rubbed his eyes in astonishment for indeed it was the very same character that he had helped carry the keg so many years ago. "Don't you know me, *Jonge*?" the little man seemed hurt.

"I do indeed," said Rip, "but I can't believe my eyes. Like the rest of me, they are failing. But it is surely you, and here we are again with so many years gone by. But you are unchanged!"

"Aye, to you it might seem that way, but to us it is as if it were yesterday, and I have aged but little in our time. Won't you join us in a game of ninepins just over the glen? You might hear the boys even from here if you haven't grown too deaf in your old age."

It was true, as Rip cupped his ear and careened his neck so as to hear better, there came the familiar clap of thunder.

"Let's be off, and why not share a pint or two to while away the hours?"

"I fear your brew and its magic my friend," Rip confessed. "But I will join you in a game, and did you say you have Wolf."

"We do! He wandered off as you slept, and he has been with us ever since."

"I must say I long to see my old companion, but how can he still be living after so many years?"

"As you yourself know, Rip Van Winkle, there is magic in these mountains. More than you might ever guess."

"Yes," said Rip, "I know it is true, and I have experienced that magic firsthand."

"You have indeed. But now let's be off before the company drinks all the beer."

When Rip did not return home that evening Judith went to the inn thinking he might have slept there that night. But he was nowhere to be found. The next day, after she pleaded with a few of the men at the inn, a party was organized to go in search of her wayward father. They spent the entire day looking for him, and as dusk settled in they gave up and returned home. Weeks passed, then a month, and by the next spring the thought of finding Rip Van Winkle had vanished as did the man himself.

It was a mild spring day when young Benjamin Franklin De Groote decided he would have another try at finding old Rip either asleep or dead. He felt sure he had returned to the mystical knoll and once again fallen asleep. Benjamin had heard Rip's story so many times he felt he could recognize the magical hill if he came upon it.

Tired and about to give up, he climbed to what he decided would be his last attempt at finding the old vagrant. Sure enough, the spot seemed perfect. Abundant in berries, soft grass, and a glorious view of the great river. It seemed to jump out from one of Rip's stories.

Searching about he suddenly heard the sound of thunder. But instead of coming from above him, it appeared to come from below, from a deep cavern and narrow pass down the mountain to a small valley. Curious he decided to discover the source of the odd thunder. As he neared the bottom he stared down at a beautiful glen, and there before his eyes was a motley crew of storybook characters playing nine pins, and among them was a disheveled old man—the spitting image of Rip Van Winkle with an old dog by his side.

He stopped in his tracks as the whole party quit their play and stared up at him. Completely undone and scared out of his wits, young Benjamin turned on his heels and ran for what he thought was his life.

The bowling party burst into laughter. It was the most emotion Rip had ever seen from them. And then they turned back to their game, that is after another helping of the mystical Catskill brew.

11

Revolution, 1838

KING WILLIAM IV WAS convinced by the British North America Company that the focus of the American colonies must remain on agriculture in the South to realize the ongoing wealth generated by the plantations, but that the North would concentrate on seeing to it that enough food, goods, services, and materials were being produced to supply the South and his rapidly growing provinces both in the north and south. The southern and northern populations were recast in the role of company employees. Any would-be citizens were censored and in several cases, tarred and feathered by company thugs.

With the phenomenal growth of the provinces, a serious turn to industrialization, especially in the North, was thought essential. The British East India Company operated as a colonial power infused with a kind of missionary zeal that seemed somehow to empower its hierarchical, paternalistic, and racist administration. Corruption was rampant. It was just as happy to make money exporting tea to China as it was opium. And the new British North America Company was following suit.

They were also xenophobic, convinced that European culture was superior to all others and that British religion and civilization were divinely appointed to reign over the rest of the world. Which is why the British North America Company tended to be less brutal and violent than its parent company. But that only held true for the white races in the American provinces. So entwined were these companies in structure, ideology, and strategy, that they commonly traded board members. Moreover, they found it expedient that their headquarters were next door to one another on London's Leadenhall Street.

Elected boards managed the companies' pooled capital, and a governor and his deputies presided over committees of oversite. Initially, they built their own ships at the dockyards at Deptford. Later they purchased them from various shipbuilders. The wealth of these two companies was such that they could afford the best-built and most well-armed fleets in the world. They ruled the seas, and their might served both the king's interests and the company's. Indeed, it was typically the case that their interests were the same. Both companies had enormous armies of British soldiers, merce-naries, and locally recruited militias, reasonably paid and loyal by threat of death. In India and North America, as well as in their holdings around the world, their authority was rarely challenged, and any revolts were put down with brutal force.

The transformation from traders to rulers began with the British East India Company where the interests of the crown and the interests of the company were so entwined that political in-volvement was certain. It was convenient and so inevitable that the companies evolved into the governing bodies of the captured territories, often acting brutally, with no hesitation to hang those suspected of rebellion or even circulating ideas of independence, freedom, or emancipation. And the companies with their fidelity to the crown left no uncertainty that George was secure in allow-ing them governance over his colonies.

In 1811 George who battled mental illness fell into a state he would not recover from, and his son George IV governed for him until his father's death in 1820. But the new king's abuse of alcohol and extravagant lifestyle led to his early death in 1830. The third son of George III, William IV, took the throne. Unlike the previous two kings, William was a temperate businessman whose faith in the two companies was unbounded. He eagerly supported their enormous control over his territories to his great benefit and the wealth of London.

The two companies were also at the forefront of the industrial revolution. Granted the industrial sector in Great Britain did not overtake the agrarian sector until 1850, nevertheless, by 1800 Britain was the most industrialized country in the world.

As the untold resources of North America began to be realized and exploited, the British North America Company began to outperform the British East India Company and profits were mounting. Previously what there was of the industrial sector amounted to not much more than gristmills and sawmills. But the company realized it needed to keep up with the growing demand for a vast assortment of old and new products beginning with food production, transportation, and the improved production of its exports. Consequently, canals and railroads were developed and expanded. Quite early and in concert with the growing focus on industrialization, the company recognized the importance of the Lehigh Valley region of Pennsylvania where mining for iron ore, steel making, and textile production were making incredible strides in manufacturing.

One remarkable London businessman, twenty-one-year-old Samuel Slater, approached the British North America Company with a plan to export British textile techniques to America. They hired him on the spot, and by 1800 they put him to work in Rhode Island. Soon his British exported innovations were dramatically improving manufacture.

"Well Moses," Slater was speaking to his assistant and confidant, Moses Brown, "I think we've put the naysayers where they belong, and they'll be eating humble pie. The few remaining company doubting Thomases have been roundly defeated, and we have assurances from the very top that we have carte blanche to build mills. Simply put, the Arkwright patterns have revolutionized the textile industry in Great Britain and North America."

Brown was an American textile executive in the pay of the British North America Company and under Slater's authority. Formerly Brown had established mills based on the old designs with modest success, so he had direct experience in building mills and hiring labor. But the company put Brown under Slater's command, and he delivered to him the patterns developed in England by Sir Richard Arkwright who was handsomely paid for the patterns to be used in North America. With the company's funding, they built six mills in Rhode Island, Massachusetts, and Connecticut. The Arkwright design included the development of the spinning or water frame so named because it was powered by water. Also, the North American mills included Arkwright's carding engine which converted raw cotton into cotton lap prior to spinning. Cotton lap were wide sheets of loosely matted cotton which were formed on the textile machine. The lap helped avoid excessive strain on the comber needles. Also, it avoided the loss of good fibers in the nods and provided a high degree of evenness in the fabric. Again, borrowing from the Arkwright method Slater combined power, machinery, semi-skilled labor, and the raw material of cotton in order to mass produce cotton yarn.

"Nothing short of brilliant," replied Moses Brown.

"I had no doubt, Moses. Company profits are soaring, and with the improvement in infrastructure the sky's the limit."

"No question about it," Brown added. "And the one problem we faced with an unskilled labor force is being overcome by experience. It was a stroke of genius on your part to create training opportunities and increased salaries for workers who showed greater aptitude. These men are indebted to the company because they see themselves as a cut above the unskilled coworkers."

"Indeed," said Slater. "I had a feeling this would come about. Just human nature, I guess. And now with Whitney on board, our industry is at the cutting age of a new mechanistic age."

He was speaking of the southern inventor, Eli Whitney, who had contacted the company at the end of the eighteenth century and proposed that they fund the development of his cotton gin. They immediately hired him, and the result was a boon to the textile industry. By the early 1800's the company turned America into the cotton capital of the world supplying 75% of the world's cotton on the backs of the enslaved.

"As it is the state of the art is our seventy-two-spindle mill in Pawtucket, Rhode Island. Whitney's cotton gin not only reduced labor costs, but also allowed for the use of short-staple cotton which grows in the upland regions. Access to cotton production on those plantations has doubled our output."

"Smartest thing they ever did next to hiring you, Slater, was bringing that Whitney fellow onboard. It's the best and the brightest leading the company in sky-high profits." Moses was prone to flattering his boss.

Gunpowder production, steam power, and a host of new inventions and technologies seemed to create the illusion of invincibility for the company. Its success meant wealth and wealth meant the continued support of the crown whose grip on power in Great Britain was unquestioned.

Out West, the most recent provinces added to King William's empire were Arkansas and Michigan, and every province was committed to maintaining slavery throughout the continent according to the King's edict and its ratification by the Tory-held parliament. As each province was officially added to the commonwealth, directors-generals were assigned to govern. But although the British were intent on claiming Texas and California for their own, Mexico also laid claim to the provinces which led to war.

In 1837 Queen Victoria ascended the throne. However, she was eighteen years old and under the thumb of her mother and her mother's lover, Sir John Conroy, one of the most powerful directors of the British North America Company, whose wealth and authority were largely due to that position. At the time of her ascension, the Tories remained in control of Parliament for an incredible eighty-three years. Robert Peel was Prime Minister since 1834 beating out a Whig favorite and close friend of Victoria, Lord Melbourne.

Victoria's temperament listed toward the Whig party, but she was severally constrained by her mother and Conroy, and when she decided to assert herself she was caught up in a scandal. She wrongfully accused Lady Flora Elizabeth Rawden-Hastings of adultery, and the Tories successfully tarnished her image and weakened her power significantly such that the British masses derided her in public. With her power in check the imperialism of the empire seemed unassailable and any ascendancy of the Whig Party unlikely.

But what the British leaders did not appreciate nor seek to fully understand was that the success they were having was empowering employees and the enslaved who longed to be free citizens. Unknown to company executives, educated northern and southern slaves and employees were being transformed by the philistine business model from property-hungry individualists of the pre-revolutionary war era to community-minded people advocating for a unified pluralism and an attitude of tolerance for differing views. The influence was profound on Frederick Douglas and became a hallmark of the ongoing African American resistance. Because they were in a sense both chattel for the company, the humiliating colonialism of the company led to a sharing of aspirations by the employees and the enslaved. And although the treatment and savagery meted out to the enslaved far exceeded what the Europeans endured, the two developed a kinship owing to their predicament. Thus, even as new provinces were added under the control of the British North America Company, employees and enslaved who dreamed of self-rule were growing in number, and they began to lose their former distrust and even hatred of one another and began to see each other as aspiring to the same goals. Whether British, Irish, Dutch, German, or African, the sense of unity in their shared vision of freedom and self-rule began to whittle away at former prejudices.

Even before the war North Americans were reading John Locke, Voltaire, and David Hume. This was as much the case for European Americans as African Americans. The French Revolution with its radical idea of egalitarianism was appealing to many. But it went hand in hand with the rise of Napoleon who naturally proved to be a distraction to Great Britain. And with the war with Mexico, the British were doubly distracted. This in turn led the way for the freedom lovers in North America to quietly conspire in underground movements unbeknownst to the London establishment.

But much more was at stake for the enslaved Blacks for whom freedom was not an abstract concept of human rights but the actual recovery of their families, the right to property and dignity, as well as their role in shaping the future of the United Provinces of North America. It was a question of empowerment, and the time was growing near. Their pending revolution found synergy in previously unallied forces. Underestimated by virtually everyone, including the polder, was a sophisticated, well-led, and impassioned resistance movement among African Americans. It was generally known that the movement with the support of white abolitionists, created an underground railroad moving and hiding enslaved people in areas where the company had less control. Typically, that was out west. Far less known by white America was that the railroad was also an intricate network of interaction within the movement. The lines of communication were part of an elaborate plan to rise up against the British North America Company and all of Great Britain.

Just as the polder was about to make their move two well-trained and organized all-black armies of the formerly enslaved and free men under the leadership of their declared supreme commander, Frederick Douglas of Maryland, prepared for battle. On June 12, 1838, Douglas declared war against Great Britain on behalf of the "free Americans of the United Provinces of North America." He summarily emancipated all enslaved people by declaration of the commander and chief of the United Provinces and proclaimed its independence from Great Britain. Their now fully exposed and well-equipped Army of the Potomac was led by General Martin Robison Delany, a former student at Harvard, a trained physician, and a close associate of Frederick Douglas. His first strength was not in warfare but rather statesmanship, but his second in command, Lieutenant General André Cailloux, a free man and business leader in New Orleans, was a self-taught strategist and military genius who read voraciously in the history of warfare. They led an army of 10,000 African American soldiers from the Columbia and Delaware territories.

The Blue Ridge Raiders were a light cavalry and infantry of four thousand men recruited from Virginia, the Carolinas, and Tennessee. Lieutenant Abraham Galloway led them. Commander Douglas ordered the two armies to lay siege to Fort Arbuthnot in South Carolina. The armies were ferried to the fort under cover of darkness by Douglas's fledgling navy under the command of Admiral Absalom Boston. In addition, Boston provided naval support for the siege. Within days of Douglas's declaration, Boston captured several British warships and assigned a task force to take as many ships as they could man. They fearlessly attacked the naval bases of the company headquarters they knew were vulnerable, and their marines took hundreds of prisoners and jailed the company directors. The enslaved were freed, and the men eagerly enlisted in the Black army which continued to swell their ranks. The newly freed women along with those women of the Underground Railroad provided logistical support in the most creative ways imaginable. Clandestine schools taught children while recruiting the older ones for service. Supply lines and artillery stations were designed and managed mostly by African American women. Captured textile mills and manufacturing plants were operated by women who supplied, among other things, uniforms for the troops.

The attack on Fort Arbuthnot was nearly bloodless as the American forces overwhelmed the incredulous British. Securing the fort and its armaments, the armies with their naval support made for Charleston across the bay and up Ashley River. From the north, a large army led by General Edward King swept down on Charleston in a two-front battle.

Immediately the polder realized this was their opportunity and opened war fronts in New York, Delaware, Pennsylvania, New Jersey, and Massachusetts. Their brigades in the South were dispatched under Lars Scholte to reinforce the African armies at Charleston but before they could arrive Charleston surrendered, and the Black forces began their march north rapidly taking

Georgetown, Wilmington, and Raleigh. Scholte met up with them in Wilmington. They targeted cities, military installations, and especially plantations, liberating any remaining enslaved who had not yet left the plantations. The sight of Black and White troops fighting in harmony with one another and successfully mounting campaign after campaign utterly unhinged the company leaders whose idea of White supremacy found the successes incomprehensible. The armies of the polder and of Douglas immediately acknowledged the ranks of their allies and followed orders as if the officers were their own. As they moved north and with word of the revolt spreading, the armies were met with significant resistance. However, by capturing the cities and plantations in the South thousands of former slaves reinforced them eager to join in the revolution. Moreover, in their planning, both the polder troops and Douglas's troops had stockpiled vast numbers of weapons including cannons. They had also created supply lines with safe storage facilities throughout the South, commandeering railroads, canals, and stagecoach routes. Many of these facilities were managed by women.

The next great offensive would combine the African armies with the army led by General Scholte. Their object was to bring down Richmond. The siege was anticipated to be a long and bloody one when suddenly the task was accomplished when the director-general was assassinated by one of the polder spies in tandem with the planned violent uprising of the city's remaining Black population who attacked the backs of the company soldiers as they manned the city's defenses. This was in conjunction with the spy network's intelligence gathering which demoralized the company soldiers and volunteers with a massive cannon barrage precisely targeting the director's office and company depots, barracks, and armory. It was followed by a conclusive frontal assault on the city and its complete surrender.

Concurrently, patriot armies under the leadership of provincial rebels from the western frontier marched east decimating the company's soldiers and holdings in the western provinces, looting and burning the offices of the British North America Company, and capturing any of the directors-general they found and putting them in jail. They too picked up supplies, armaments, equipment, and volunteers as they marched east. As they advanced they were constantly reinforced by the legendary African Buffalo Soldiers who left everything behind to join in the revolt against Great Britain. Their heroism and bravery were unsurpassed. Even at the sight of them, numbers of company soldiers turned on their employers recognizing the change of wind and anticipating the demise of the British North America Company.

The specific task of the western front was to destroy the company's presence in the northern provinces, and they were aided by the formerly clandestine militias under the command of the leaders of the polder, while the African American troops focused on taking down the southern cities. Consequently, the formerly all-Black armies, which now included a multi-racial mix, turned south again.

They marched looting and burning the remaining Loyalist and company plantations and forced the White families south. The former slaveholders dared not try to blend in with the growing number of White sympathizers, as they were easily identified by the freed slaves who were by and large part of the American armies. However, the Loyalists recognized that if the revolt was successful it meant the end of colonialism and their way of life in so far as it depended for its existence on slavery. Their options were to flee south, surrender, or join up with the company soldiers. As they made their way south many of the men did just that, they sent the women and children on their way and joined up with company regulars. This amounted to serious resistance to the African troops. However, harboring deep resentment of the company, they were typically half-hearted in their efforts. While they fought alongside the company's soldiers, they were loath to risk their lives and tended to obey orders only to a point. Many deserted finding the horrific losses intolerable. Soon, rather than join the rebellion or die alongside the company soldiers, most of them simply fled south and west to join up with their families and sit out the war hoping the British would prevail. But the Black tide was advancing.

Douglas was now in charge of four well-equipped and battle-hardened armies. From Richmond, they marched west to Raleigh and Charlotte, and having already taken Charleston, they moved on to Colombia and finally to Savanna in the Province of Georgia. As they marched they pushed a massive migration of Loyalist families in front of them as they fled to the south and west. Having sacked Savanna and left it burning, the armies turned northwest in order to come up behind the fleeing Loyalists and company men. Meanwhile, Scholte and his army proceeded south to sandwich the enemy between their two forces in a successful rout of the remnants of the company's troops. Now the combined armies turned north again and marched for New York where the major fear was the formidable British Navy. If the rebellion was to fail it would be at the hands of the greatest navy in the world.

The synergism of the revolt was catastrophic for British morale as if a tsunami was rolling over the entire continent. Meanwhile, world events were lining up against Great Britain both globally and at home. Alexander Dallas Bache, Benjamin Franklin's great-grandson, who had been in exile in France, negotiated French support from Napoleon III at the request of the polder. He then traveled to the Netherlands with an urgent request penned by Lars Scholte and cosigned by Frederick Douglas requesting Dutch naval assistance. The Dutch Navy had suffered catastrophic losses and ceded most of its power and influence certainly after the Fourth Dutch-Anglo War of 1780-1784. It had been absorbed by the French Navy. But now they were rebuilding, and with the French coming to the aid of the rebels in America the recovering Dutch fleet, which was mostly situated in East Asia at the time, was ordered out of Asia and off to North America with orders to blockade the crucial southern points of entry into the country's interior. They situated their ships in a fairly effective net to cover the Mississippi at New Orleans, the Chesapeake near Norfolk, the Delaware Bay, Cape Fear near Southport, and Charleston Harbor. However, they were not willing to pursue any British ships that successfully ran the blockade, but they fired on all British ships that challenged them, and it certainly reduced British presence in the American interior to the extent that they could not mount a serious challenge to the uprising.

On December 3rd, 1841, the French Fleet entered New York Harbor dispatching an army of 10,000 legionnaires. New York fell in three days' time. Director-general William Hedge was ordered to surrender the city unconditionally. He responded that he could not do that without permission from the crown. A ship was dispatched with the terms of surrender of the entirety of British North America. Meanwhile, the French and a courageous if randomly led armada of hidden and seized ships crewed by Black and White seamen, defended New York Harbor.

Instead of surrendering Queen Victoria was coerced into sending a fleet of well-armed British ships to New York with orders to retake the city and destroy the rebels. They arrived on March 15, 1842. But the fleet was weakened because so many of their ships were still committed to the war with France and Mexico. The fleet of one hundred warships was met by Admiral Boston's armada of an equal number and the French force of sixty ships. The fighting was furious but eventually New York militias were able to board the battered British vessels and commandeer the ships turning their guns on the enemy. With the hoisting of a flag designed by Harriet Tubman on a green background with thirty-one yellow stars beginning in the lower right-hand corner and moving upward, one for each of the free provinces, Boston and the French ceased their fire and focused on the remaining British ships. New York fell by the end of the month. Meanwhile, the armies from the western provinces quadrupled as they marched east picking up thousands upon thousands of former employees of the British North America Company and arming them.

With the defeat of the British Navy and the march eastward of the Western militias, the Northern troops of the polder and their allies devastated what remained of the company's resistance in the North. Meanwhile, the armies of Douglas turned around and marched on Baltimore, supported by Boston's navy. Surrounded and besieged, the company directors dug in for a long fight. They demanded reinforcements from London, but in spite of pressure from her mother, Victoria refused. Parliament was invoked to overrule the queen even as the Tories were soundly defeated in the elections of 1842. For the first time in most people's memory, the Whigs assumed power supported by a queen who was proving herself formidable. With the parliamentary election behind her, she sued for peace with the full support of the Whig majority, the only condition being that the remaining company leaders and soldiers be allowed safe passage by ship to England. The entirety of the British North America Company was recalled and hastily sought passage on British ships commissioned to ferry the survivors back to England. In the summer of 1842, the Third Continental Congress met in New York City and drafted a preliminary constitution for consideration and a vote by the United Provinces of North America.

12

President Delany, 1842

AT THE MEETING OF the Third Continental Congress in New York
City in August 1842, chosen representatives from the thirty-one
provinces gathered at the old Dutch church on Garden Street.
Where political structures existed in the provinces they were
elected by ballot. Where the structures were not yet in place
representatives were simply appointed. Several others were in at-
tendance serving as staff support for the representatives, but each
province was given one vote on all matters before the Congress
regardless of the size of the province, and all of the provinces were
represented. Frederick Douglas was elected president pro-tempore
and Lars Scholte was elected clerk of the Congress. Neither wished
to remain in office beyond the upcoming general election, which
would be held once a constitution was ratified. New York was declared the capital of the United Provinces of North America. It fell
to Douglas to prepare the first draft of the Constitution. It proved
to be a lengthy document filled with details of the various branches
and the processes that would guide them. However, briefly sum-
marize, Douglas took as his initial template the documents from
the previous meetings of the Continental Congress, beginning
with the Declaration of Independence and Preamble. However,
having covered the prewar documents, he deviated considerably
from the earlier course of Congress and drew heavily from his own

writings and convictions. He worked hand in hand with a small number of polder members and southern delegates always seeking their views. As such, the Preamble began by skipping the original July 4th Declaration's opening paragraph defending its reason for separating from Great Britain and went instead directly to the Lockean-inspired words about self-evident truths which included universal equality and the right to life, liberty, and the pursuit of property. But Douglas added substantially to the Preamble and articles based on his own ideas.

The Constitution held that all nations are under God's care; that God intended the leaders to seek the flourishing of all humankind. Therefore, the standard for the government and the country would be primarily a moral one, with economic interests having a secondary role. Hence, the markets were meant to be used in the service of God and not in their own interests. And although the right to private property would be protected by law, it remained subordinate to the public good.

The Preamble went on to assert that in order for humanity to flourish avarice must be kept in check as it will only impede the design of God for all people to obtain salvation. Likewise, the pursuit of wealth over the care of the working population was an offense to God and must be prohibited by the government of the United Provinces. Profit would not be permitted to trump justice, freedom, and equal opportunity for all. However, the country would not establish any particular church or faith.

Again, skipping the references to the previous "Abuses" and "Usurpations" of the British, Douglas next moved to the declaration of the sovereignty and legitimacy of the newly formed United Provinces of North America, and the commitment of all the provinces to defend the republic against any hostile powers by supporting a standing militia. The executive branch would oversee the maintenance of a navy.

Article One was primarily a declaration of rights, which began with the assertion of equality before the law and the prohibition of discrimination. The right to vote was granted to every male citizen above the age of twenty-one, as well as the right to petition the government. Religious freedom was guaranteed to all citizens, as was freedom of speech. This was also granted to the press, "in order that a conscience keep watch over the decision-makers." Douglas included the right to freedom of association and assembly. He secured the right to privacy and property. Finally, he included the right to liberty making it a crime to unlawfully detain a citizen.

Article Two spelled out the duties of the Executive Branch of the government. He was to be elected for a four-year term with no ability to run a second time. Any party able to hold a convention could select a candidate by vote of the assembly to attend the national convention along with any members of Congress from the same party. Also attending was the delegate chosen to nominate the candidate. The candidates would attend the convention in New York City scheduled for September 1844, if the Constitution was duly ratified, and would be held six months prior to the national election. The participants would then debate the qualifications of the nominees. The former clerk of the Congress would chair the election. A vote could be called at any time by a motion, a second, and the approval of two thirds of the assembly. The vote would then be taken and the candidate receiving a majority of the votes would be eligible to run for president. A second debate would then be held in order to decide who would be the second candidate under the same conditions. The second candidate must be from a different party. Having two candidates selected to run for the office of president, a general election for the whole country would be held. The candidate receiving the majority in each province would receive the support of that province which would be one electoral vote. When all the provinces had voted the candidate with the most electoral votes became president. In the unlikelihood of a tie the former clerk would decide the election. The candidate having the minority of votes became vice president with no other duty then to fill the office of president should he die or be found guilty of a serious crime by the senate.

Douglas designed this system intending to reduce party politics as much as possible and create a system of unselfish service among politicians. He also shrewdly recognized the reasonable cost associated with this election process with the expenses being evenly distributed among both the federal and provincial governments. Again, this would deter attempts to buy an election.

The president-elect would then appoint his clerk and a council to aid him in his various duties. Each member of the Executive Council would have a distinct responsibility such as the War Office or Treasury. Council appointees had to be approved by the Senate.

Article Three described the Congress of the United Provinces, having a House of Representatives and a Senate. Legislators were chosen by a popular election in their province for four-year terms. Each province had one member of the house and one senator. The duties of the House were to make and pass federal laws and modify and repeal those laws in order to defend the interests of the citizens. The Senate would advise and give consent to treaties and to presidential appointments. It would try and impeach officials accused and found guilty of a crime. A great deal more material spelled out the nature of those duties and the processes of both the House and Senate in more detail. Each province would have a House of Representatives and a Senate whose duties were essentially the same as the national Congress except they applied to the provinces.

Article Four concerned the judiciary. Douglas was keen to see to it that the Judicial Branch be independent of the executive and legislative branches. The High Court would protect the Constitution and hear appeals from the lower provincial courts. The Federal Courts would interpret the law according to the Constitution. Provincial courts would do the same for the provinces.

That very briefly summarized, was the outline of Douglas's government. At their second meeting the following year, the New York delegates debated the Constitution, made substantial changes primarily clarifying the governmental processes which increased its size considerably, and passed a resolution to pass it on to the provinces for ratification.

As the country began to heal from the war, energetic political debate was being renewed. The popularity of the Whig platform was to be expected, and yet Americans were seeking a new political identity of their own. The polder was emerging as a strong party of its own, and its character was significantly different from the Whig platform. Philosophically, it rejected popular British philosophical realism and Victorian propriety. They preferred the idealism of the German schools of thought and eschewed elitist and nationalistic agendas.

However, while the contents of Douglas's Constitution to some extent mirrored the philosophy behind it, it was Douglas's larger vision that would be reflected in the presidency of the second United Provinces president, the war hero Martin Robison Delany, Douglas's student in statecraft. Delany echoed his mentor's views. Of course, Douglas was most famous for his writings on abolition. Before most others, he declared slavery a sin and a blight on all humanity. And he was tireless in his campaign to rid the world of its curse. He scoffed at the early ideas of repatriation insisting that America was the only country most of the enslaved ever knew, and how was it that except for the badly treated Indigenous, there should be a group that were more "American" than others. "Might we send our Irish back to Ireland, our English back to England, and our Germans back to Germany? What an afront to reason, and beyond reason the height of unjust and immoral thinking."

But far less known except to people like Delany, were his writings on social and political philosophy. While he admired the work of John Locke he entirely turned his back on British empiricism and wrote vigorously against popular Scottish Common-Sense Realism. Instead, with his friends in the now fully formed Polder Party, Douglas embraced something he called "practical idealism." It was heavily informed by German philosophy but avoided their penchant for abstraction. It had its Romantic influences, but it was not a blanket rejection of reason as the essential tool for social and industrial progress. Thus, it had a strong commitment to praxis of the activist sort.

In outlining his philosophy Douglas wrote in distinction to British philosophy, especially its theory of the mind and how it works, that the mind's operations are not of the mechanistic sort, composed of individual faculties that work in harmony like the parts of a watch. These so-called "faculties" were in fact interdependent. The mind, wrote Douglas, is "an organic union of these mental faculties which are self-engaged and self-engaging in processes of distinction and unity, an organic process of unseen preexistent forces." For example, he spoke of the way the acorn became the oak by virtue of an invisible power within it, and he insisted that all of life is directed by that same unseen natural law or power. It was a theory of natural development from an organic perspective, and Douglas applied his modern teleological theory to history as well.

By way of his idealism and its analogies, Douglas insisted on the organic interdependence of all of life, "from the clod to the human soul." All of life was animated by a plastic power which guided the development of nature and spirit.

In a brilliant series published in the *National Review*, Douglas insisted that mechanical theories of life cannot capture the full dimensions and complexity of life. Nor can they bring together the worlds of spirit and nature as they were meant to be. The realists' bent is toward the natural, and so they distort the phenomena of nature altogether. For Douglas the unseen or spiritual (he would sometimes say "supernatural") world is in full harmony with the natural world. As such, he eschewed the dualism of realist thinking which would pit nature against spirit. Rather he insisted on "a dialectic approach which recognizes the physical and spiritual as constituting different sides of one reality. Only as we keep this in mind do we avoid on the one hand, a culture steeped in mythology and gnostic delusion, an inert culture without the benefit of science to advance civilization, and on the other hand a grossly materialistic society concerned exclusively with acquisition." In a brilliant summary of his position Douglas wrote, "It is the height of folly to make the sphere of nature the ultimate source of knowledge. Can we be so naïve as to think the moral interests of our new nation can be subjugated by material interests? Have we not learned from the struggles we have endured by the demonic institution of slavery, which was governed by greed, not to have realized that profit must not rule our minds. And have we not realized notwithstanding the enormous strides and advances made by science and technology, that commerce has too often been wielded to an evil design in order to benefit a minority? To deceive ourselves into thinking that our nation will achieve its brilliance solely by means of mechanics and by material laws of nature and physics, by chemistry, geology, and other such sciences. To apply their harnessed powers exclusively to be used by business and trade? No, this cannot be. There is a greater purpose beyond which the science of nature is wed to the study of mind such that we come to realize that we do not seek to engineer ourselves. It is here, as we understand ourselves as ensouled beings, utterly interdependent and made in the image of God, that we begin the ascent for which we were created and destined to find our consummation. In the study of mind and nature as mutually interdependent we recognize the sacramental mystery of our existence, and having done so the divine will find its place in nature and at once nature will find its place in the divine."

Douglas's practical idealism was at the heart of Polder Party thinking, and its philosophical orientation became the foundation of the party's platform. That became evident in their insistence on remaining on the gold standard, having a strong central bank carefully monitored by the Department of the Treasury, both thought to check the greed of a growing number of enormously wealthy industrialists. In addition, they wished to pursue the cause of woman's suffrage, maintain peace with Mexico, and the fair treatment of the Indigenous. They sought to limit the size of the navy and military as a purely defensive force. They resisted unrestrained nationalistic expansionism, insisting on a model of slow and well-planned growth of both the agricultural and industrial sectors by way of collaboration with all the legitimate parties and their supporters.

But the Dutch influence was also felt in their long history of commerce. The Polder Party called for an immediate acceleration in shipbuilding and sea trade. They denounced protectionism and insisted on limited use of tariffs, saying that free trade would be a boon to the nation's economy. They advocated for industrial growth, but under the control of a Department of Economic Development which would also protect workers' safety and wages.

Most interesting, however, was the Polder's rejection of a political pluralism that might lead to legislative standoffs. They advocated for a dispassionate pluralism where parties were obliged to seek understanding and consensus among themselves, recognizing that the party in power would lead the discussion and bring healthy debate to a conclusion. Congress would seek to make decisions based on consensus building for economic and social policy making. The Department of Economic Development would oversee and guide conversations between labor interests and employer organizations.

At this point in time political parties were not strictly organized but rather existed as a group of citizens with a shared agenda. Any voting citizen could attend the party conventions and participate. Douglas was still aligned with the Freedom Party whose entire platform was fixed on bringing the formerly enslaved Americans fully into the mainstream of American life. While popular with the Black population, many felt its vision was too narrow and lacked ideas that would advance the economic interests of the country.

The Whig Party was popular among educated White American males who shared a Victorian sense of decorum. They were strong on personal conduct, evangelical in their religion, and somewhat elitist in their view of the working population. They were fierce advocates of military might, expansion into the West, and gaining territory in Central America. And although they desired a central bank, they did not see the need to closely monitor its dealings. But shortly after the ratification of the Constitution the party began to fracture, and many of them eschewed the social agenda of the British Whigs adopting instead several old Tory positions. They began to argue that unions would restrain productivity and produce insolent workers, and that too much regulation would threaten economic growth. They utterly rejected suffrage on all counts, and would advance an amendment to the Constitution that voters must be educated property owners. Most of the growing number of industrialists were New Whigs. Also, they were rabid expansionists. Old Whig's were less enthusiastic about expansion, they were not overly nationalistic, and while both were conservative in their lifestyle, Old Whig's had more interest in social issues while New Whigs were focused on economics and keen on industrialization, capitalism, and private property.

While these were the leading parties, several other parties came and went. A small number of former southern plantation owners became politically active in the cause of rebuilding the devastated South. They became the Reconstruction Party. While it had considerable influence in the South, again its lack of a comprehensive plan for the whole nation weakened it. There was a small woman's suffrage party but again, without the vote and having a small number of males as members, its power was exclusively in raising the issue. They struggled to hold a convention.

In effect, the United Provinces' form of government was a federal republic which insured provincial rights to an extent with multiple parties whose power depended on electing presidents and congressmen. The strength or weakness of the provinces versus the executive was a question never fully resolved and executive verses state's powers would continue to be debated for years to come. Executive power would vacillate back and forth depending on public opinion and the decisions and effectiveness of the nation's leaders.

When the central tenants of the Freedom Party were added to the Polder Party along with southern reconstruction, Douglas switched his support to the Polder and Delany joined him. Delany was chosen as their candidate for president at their convention in 1843 which shortly followed the ratification of the Constitution on the first ballot. The Whigs fought among themselves and divided their vote between Cleveland Marshall and Barton Albright. Marshall was a millionaire industrialist with strong ties to the New Whig agenda. Albright was a popular Whig in the tradition of Edmund Burke filled with Victorian sensitivities, manners, and sentiment. After several ballots Marshall narrowly won the party's nomination.

The Freedom Party managed to hold a successful convention and nominated John Bathan Vashon, a seaman and old abolitionist. But with the defection of Douglas, the party lost much of its influence and many of its supporters. Still, Vashon remained a strong candidate in the nomination process.

The general election was held in March 1845, and the result was a resounding victory for Delany and the Polder Party. African American turnout was at nearly one hundred percent, while the old Whig's balked at supporting Albright. Delany took office on April 23, 1845. The course for America was now set by a revolutionary concept of the freedom and rights of all individuals within the bounds of the law. But perhaps most fascinating for the new nation itself was the unexpected virtual canonizing of former slaves, which intensified as their aging numbers dwindled by death. The "remnant" as they were called, were revered and treated with holy respect as eyewitnesses to the atrocities of enslavement. Many wrote books, lectured, toured the country, and led religious services and memorials. The sense for most in the country was that as long as they lived they were a monument to those who were subjugated and brutalized for the greed of men.

13

A Catskill Village, 1845

KILIAEN VAN TWILLER TURNED the key to his shop's door and opened it. It was midmorning, opening time. It stood out as an oddity in the small Catskill Village for its architecture. It was one of the few remaining authentically Dutch colonial houses with its brickwork, latices, gables, and weather cock. There were few such houses still standing, most torn down and replaced by modest Cape Cods or stately Victorian homes. Also peculiar was that it was surrounded by a hedge labyrinth decorated with realistic looking ghosts, goblins, fiendish scarecrows, tombstones, and convincingly rendered bats made authentic by expert taxidermists, hanging from their claws in the surrounding trees. The sign at the entrance to the labyrinth and shop read "Catskills Shop of Mysteries."

Like the house, Kiliaen was an oddity. The ancestral Dutch were almost gone or had married beyond the Knickerbocker tribes such that they knew little of their own history and language. Kiliaen was the last of a dying breed swept away by the overwhelming tide of inevitable assimilation. The Dutch had long since ceased any meaningful migration to the North American Provinces, and their remaining influence was subtle. For example, rivers and streams still carried the word "kill" in them such as the Beaverkill, the Dutch meaning being a body of water. The Catskills got their name from Wildcat Creek. Roads and bridges retained their historic titles, and much of the flora had Dutch names like the daffodil. What also remained of ancient Dutch culture were many of the old legends and superstations. Many of the practices around the time of Halloween were handed down from Dutch as well as English traditions, including pumpkin carving, telling ghost stories, roasting apples, and visiting haunted houses.

Kiliaen's little curiosity shop was fairly successful relying on the reasonable tourist revenues generated by visitors taken with the legend of Rip Van Winkle, along with the now famous tales and stories of the mysterious Catskill Mountains. He sold books based on the old legends and souvenirs, mostly manufactured in China, claiming local authenticity. You could buy the ordinary run of the mill items such as wampum, Indian arrowheads, and beaver pelts. Or you could spend serious money purchasing a love potion, a totem used for curses, or a map of where Rip Van Winkle was said to have fallen asleep. More practically you could buy a pair of Dutch knickers, a swath of homespun, or a pair of moccasins. There were eagle feathers said to be identical to the one worn by Rip Van Winkle himself. And if you really fancied the bats, ghosts, and tombstones in the labyrinth, they were on offer as well.

For an even steeper fee you could hire a guide to take you on a tour of the village and visit the site of the former home of the Van Winkle family. Or you could enjoy a draft of Old Delft at The George near the great hearth or in the beer garden beneath the old sycamore tree. Story tellers and minstrels entertained the tourists, and for a hefty fee they could be taken to the very spot from which Rip allegedly disappeared along with the site of the famous game of nine pins.

Less than an hour after opening Kiliaen heard the bell attached to the shop's door ring. He knew without looking it was his old friend and frequent visitor Pieter Van Winkle, Rip's grandson. He made his living taking tourists on guided tours as well as producing many of the items sold at the Catskill Shop of Mysteries. It was said he could stitch a pair of moccasins better than the natives.

While Kiliaen fiddled around in the back of the store scavenging for more items to display, Pieter set up the checkerboard. "No tours today, Pieter?" Kiliaen inquired.

"Nay, with it being late fall the cold has put them off. Can't say as I blame them. No matter, it just gives me more time stitching moccasins. In fact, I have to take the wagon over to Tarrytown this afternoon to buy some skins. I'm all out. You and I did some serious business last summer. I had to stitch up some size twelves. Never had to do that before. Imagine, men with such big feet."

"Aye, the souvenirs really took off last season. But by my reckoning you were kept busy runnin' tourists out to Blueberry Perch." The perch got its name from the abundance of blueberries in the area, although whether it was the same high point where Rip fell asleep was in dispute. There were several such nolls with amazing views of the Hudson. It was true, however, that just below and slanting west from Blueberry Perch was a rugged ravine leading to a small grassy valley. Naturally, Kiliaen and Pieter swore to its authenticity, but they had a vested interest. Nobody really knew for sure.

"I been meaning to ask you, Kiliaen, up there, top shelf left, above the old muskets and war memorabilia, there's a half dozen flags and about the same number of busts of some fellow prayin'. They been there since I know'd yer shop, but never have I seen any of 'em get sold. Is that why they're way up top and almost out of sight?"

"Aye," Kiliaen replied. "Don't want to waste good space on those. Never sold a one. Never ordered any more of 'em either."

"Well, what's the flag and who's the fellow on his knees? Seems he's in some uniform or another?" came Pieter's response.

"The flag's from the first revolution where the American's got whopped by the British. Supposed to be made by a Betsy Ross. The thirteen stars were the old colonies. But nobody recognizes it, nor do they seem to care. Been asked only two or three times about 'em."

"What about the prayin' man?"

"Oh, that's supposed to be General George Washington, praying at Valley Forge. Same thing though, nobody seems interested. Most don't even know the name. But I'm too preoccupied to bring them down, and I don't have to go up there after them, so I just let 'em be to gather dust. I guess you could say they're space fillers. Gives the shelf a busy antique look."

"Aye, it's a regular museum you're runnin' here," Pieter laughed.

"Give me hand with this box will you, you loafer?" Kiliaen bristled. "I can't pull it out of the closet by myself. I got a dozen old cannon balls in there. They sell like wildfire, don't ask me why. Anything having to do with guns and weapons are big sellers."

"OK, but mind my back. Not what it used to be. Not since I tripped up by Blueberry and rolled halfway down the ravine." Pieter still walked with a cane after that fiasco.

"Listen, why don't you put down that box and come play a game of checkers," Pieter insisted. "I don't have much time before I head over to Tarrytown. I tell you what. We play a game, I go get them skins, and then I come back to help with the box. That'd be about closin' time, and we could head over to The George for some Old Delft? What do you say to that?"

"Oh, alright," was Kiliaen's reply. I shoulda know'd you'd find an excuse not to lift the box. Gonna be slow here anyway. You got that board set up yet?"

"Aye, what's it to be, black or red?" Pieter never failed to ask.

"Same as always, and ye know'd it. Black."